"Am I On The Air?" He Asked.

It was Jack Montrose! Lauren had no idea what to say. "No. I thought you didn't listen to my show."

"Good. I'm not much on being in the public eye. But once I met you I had to give it a listen. I was right about your voice. Between that and those seductive songs you play, you've been driving me out of my mind all night."

It didn't help matters that she'd spent the entire evening thinking of him as the slow sensual songs played out. "They were all requests. Do you have one?"

"No. I called to talk to you. To have you to myself for a few short minutes."

She couldn't respond to that. It was as if he'd looked into her soul and glimpsed the part she'd always hidden. She wanted to be some man's late-night fantasy....

Dear Reader,

Welcome to another fabulous month of novels from Silhouette Desire. Our DYNASTIES: THE ASHTONS continuity continues with Kristi Gold's *Mistaken for a Mistress.* Ford Ashton sets out to find the truth about who really murdered his grandfather and believes the answers may lie with the man's mistress—but who is Kerry Roarke *really?* *USA TODAY* bestselling author Jennifer Greene is back with a stellar novel, *Hot to the Touch.* You'll love this wounded veteran hero and the feisty female whose special touch heals him.

TEXAS CATTLEMAN'S CLUB: THE SECRET DIARY presents its second installment with *Less-than-Innocent Invitation* by Shirley Rogers. It seems this millionaire rancher has to keep tabs on his ex-girlfriend by putting her up at his Texas spread. Oh, poor girl…trapped with a sexy—wealthy—cowboy! There's a brand-new KING OF HEARTS book by Katherine Garbera as the mysterious El Rey's matchmaking attempts continue in *Rock Me All Night.* Linda Conrad begins a compelling new miniseries called THE GYPSY INHERITANCE, the first of which is *Seduction by the Book.* Look for the remaining two novels to follow in September and October. And finally, Laura Wright winds up her royal series with *Her Royal Bed.* There's lots of revenge, royalty and romance to be enjoyed.

Thanks for choosing Silhouette Desire. In the coming months be sure to look for titles by authors Peggy Moreland, Annette Broadrick and the incomparable Diana Palmer.

Happy reading!

Melissa Jeglinski

Melissa Jeglinski
Senior Editor
Silhouette Desire

Please address questions and book requests to:
Silhouette Reader Service
U.S.: 3010 Walden Ave., P.O. Box 1325, Buffalo, NY 14269
Canadian: P.O. Box 609, Fort Erie, Ont. L2A 5X3

Rock Me
All Night

Katherine Garbera

Published by Silhouette Books
America's Publisher of Contemporary Romance

This book is dedicated to Beverly Brandt—
thanks for the friendship and the laughter
and most especially for your rendition of
Barry Manilow's greatest hits!

SILHOUETTE BOOKS

ISBN 0-373-76672-6

ROCK ME ALL NIGHT

Copyright © 2005 by Katherine Garbera

Visit Silhouette Books at www.eHarlequin.com

Printed in U.S.A.

Books by Katherine Garbera

Silhouette Desire

The Bachelor Next Door #1104
Miranda's Outlaw #1169
Her Baby's Father #1289
Overnight Cinderella #1348
Baby at His Door #1367
Some Kind of Incredible #1395
The Tycoon's Temptation #1414
The Tycoon's Lady #1464
Cinderella's Convenient Husband #1466
Tycoon for Auction #1504
Cinderella's Millionaire #1520
In Bed with Beauty #1535
Cinderella's Christmas Affair #1546
Let It Ride #1558
Sin City Wedding #1567
Mistress Minded #1587
Rock Me All Night #1672

Silhouette Bombshell

Exposed #10
Night Life #23
The Amazon Strain #43

*King of Hearts

KATHERINE GARBERA

has had fun working as a production page, lifeguard, secretary and VIP tour guide, but those occupations pale when compared to creating worlds where true love conquers all and wounded hearts are healed. Writing romance novels is the perfect job for her.

Prologue

This afterlife gig kept getting crazier.

I'd been a capo in the mob. Actually the boss of bosses, *Il Re*. That's Italian for The King, and believe me I acted as if I owned the world. Five shots to the chest and I ended up here in that gray area Father Dom called Purgatory. It's not quite how I'd always pictured it, but then little in my experience ever was.

I'd cut a deal with one of God's emissaries, one of the seraphim with a name that was a mouthful. I'd shortened it to Didi. She had an attitude and awful taste in clothing, but something about her got to me.

"Welcome back, Pasquale."

My given name is Pasquale Mandetti, and no one but this angel broad ever got away with calling me it. "Babe, I've asked you to call me Ray."

"And I've asked you not to call me babe."

"Bad habit."

She watched me carefully. I leaned back in the leather chair that I knew was just here for show and waited. Didi played the same kind of games I used to when I'd been the boss. But she was my boss now. The deal I'd cut was to unite in love as many couples as enemies I'd murdered in hate.

Madon', do you have any idea how long I'm going to be working this matchmaking gig!

A large stack of file folders appeared on her desk. The folders were different colored, and I'd learned from experience that none of the couples were easy to get together. There was a reason why they were in a file on Didi's desk, and usually that reason was they needed more than a nudge at a willing person of the opposite sex.

"Pick a color," she said.

"Just give me the one on top," I said. I hated it when she got cute with me.

She handed me the file, and I flipped it open. Not a bad gig. I was going to be a DJ at a top-100 radio station in Detroit…in February. "I'm going to freeze my butt off."

"Probably. I'll be going with you this time."

"Why?"

"You'll need a producer. Besides, this one needs careful handling."

I skimmed the descriptions. Lauren Belchoir and Jack Montrose. They lived on opposite ends of town and had totally different lives. Jack owned a record company and Lauren worked the midnight shift at the radio station. It seemed pretty straightforward to me.

"Why do I need you along again?"

"Because you're doing the new morning drive show and you'll be in charge of the first annual Mile of Men promotion."

"What is that?"

"It's a Valentine's Day promotion where single men line up and then women drive by and pick a guy."

"And Lauren's going to pick Jack?"

"If I gave you all the answers, you wouldn't have a job to do," she said with that tricky smile of hers that I didn't trust.

I felt my body dissolve. Soon I was standing on the street looking up at a tall mirrored building. The radio call letters were plastered to the side—WCPD. *Madon',* what had I gotten myself into?

One

The meeting was long and boring. Lauren Belchoir leaned back in her chair and wished she were anyplace but here. She loved her job as the late-night DJ at WCPD and had been doing her Miss Lonely Hearts show for five years now. But suddenly they had a new program manager and everything was changing.

The new guy, Ray King, and his producer, Didi Sera, were going to shake things up and take WCPD from the bottom of Detroit's radio stations to the top. "The project is simple. A Mile of Men promotion that will entice the city's most eligible bachelors to participate. Didi is handing out folders to each of you with the men we'd like to get on our mile."

Lauren opened hers up and sucked in a breath. Jack Montrose. He was dark and attractive and had a reputation for never staying with anything for more than six months. Not a woman, a hobby or a house. He moved like lightning, living his life in the same large manner his father, Diamond Dave Montrose, had before his death.

She flipped through the rest of the folder, surprised to see her boss, Ty Montrose, in there as well. Ty and Jack were brothers. "Each of you will be assigned a bachelor to talk to. We want these men because they'll bring us publicity."

Lauren flipped through the rest of the pictures and saw Joe Brigg, the union leader of the local auto-plant workers. She already knew Joe and had in fact had dinner with him two weeks ago. Though the two of them hadn't had any chemistry, Lauren knew she could talk Joe into participating. "I know Joe Brigg, so I'll contact him."

Ray glanced over at her, his light eyes shrewd and calculating. Or was she imagining things? She scarcely knew the man. "Didi and I will take care of Joe. Lauren, I want you to contact Jack Montrose."

"But he's Ty's brother. Can't Ty talk to him?"

Ty looked uncomfortable and Lauren regretted the suggestion. They were all aware that if ratings didn't go up, then they were in trouble. And Ty was the owner, so he was in the hot seat. "It was just a suggestion."

"I think it would be better for you to handle Jack," Ray said.

Lauren knew she wasn't going to convince him to change his mind. "Whatever."

"What he means is that Ty will be busy securing the venue and organizing the bios for the men," Didi said. She sat next to Ray, her presence calming in a way that his wasn't. She wore a dove-gray suit, and her hair hung in shining waves down her back.

Lauren nodded.

"That's all for now. Except that we will be switching some of your slots around. Marshall, instead of doing afternoons I want you to take the midnight show. Lauren, I want you in the morning drive-time slot."

Lauren didn't want to move. She liked her quiet little world where she could play what she wanted and talk to her listeners. But she'd made enough waves for one meeting. Ty reached under the table and squeezed her hand reassuringly. She smiled at him.

The conference room cleared out, but Lauren lingered. Ray stood at one end talking to Didi and Marshall. Finally Marshall left and Lauren approached the new DJ and program manager.

"Can we talk?"

"Sure thing. What's up?"

"I...listen, I don't want to move to the morning slot. My listeners and I have a bond."

Didi responded without looking up from her papers. "We know. You have the highest-rated show on WCPD. In fact, the only time slot that we beat every other station in is yours."

Lauren hadn't realized her show was so popular. The previous GM had scarcely spoken to her. Which was exactly how she liked it.

"That's why we need you in the morning," Ray said.

She nodded. She knew she was fighting a losing battle with the change. "I hope my style works in the morning."

"It will," Didi said, gathering up her papers and starting for the door.

Ray hung back. "Are we square now?"

"No. I still think Ty should contact his brother."

"I've already told him to expect your call, Lauren."

"Between you and Jack, we'll be able to play up the battle of the sexes. Especially if we get Jack on board," Ray said.

"What do you mean?"

"Well, you're all home and family, that quiet sense of belonging, and he's not. He's a rogue. He lives life like it's a game. I think it's just what we need."

"I'm not good with that type of man."

"Babe, it's not about you and him. It's about ratings."

She could understand ratings. If they didn't start doing better, the radio station would be closed down. So in the end this was for her job.

Ray put his arm around her, hugging her close to his side for a minute. "I wouldn't have given you this assignment if I didn't have confidence you were the right one."

He gave her a charming smile, and she saw a bit of mischief in it. "You're heavy-handed when you want your way, aren't you?"

"Babe, you have no idea," he said, winking at her. He led her down the hall to the reception area.

"Pat, Ty needs you to help him set up the conference room for the interviewees," Ray said to the station's receptionist as they approached the front of the building.

The radio station had a nice faux cherrywood reception area. Ty said it gave visitors the impression that WCPD was a top radio station. In fact, the opposite was true. Their ratings were down and the station was desperate to do something—anything—to change that. Hence this year's Mile of Men promotion for Valentine's Day.

Pat Mallery had been at the station longer than anyone else. She could have gone on to be an office manager or probably even the station manager, but she liked being up front where things happened and gossip flowed. Lauren liked the older woman.

"Sure thing, boss. What about the phones?" Pat asked.

Ray glanced at her.

"No. I…can't," Lauren said.

Ray shrugged, glancing past her before sitting down. "No problem. I've got them."

Lauren hurried down the hall, away from the strange new guy who was now their program manager. She bumped into someone and looked up to apologize. The man standing before her had eyes the same color as the winter sky, cold and icy. His hair was thick and black but starting to gray at the temples. His shoulders were broad and his suit had an expensive cut to it. Jack Montrose.

"Sorry," she said, realizing she'd been staring at him for too long.

"My fault. I wasn't paying attention," he said. His low, deep voice brushed over her senses like sunlight on a cold day, bringing them all to life.

Damn. She felt little shivers spread down her neck. She had a thing for deep voices. Maybe it was from working in radio for so long. This man's voice was the kind dreams were made of. She'd give good money to listen to him reading sonnets to her by a crackling fire.

He still held her shoulder where he'd reached out to steady her. She felt his heat through the thin layer of her silk shirt. She wished now she'd worn her Gore-Tex vest over the shirt this morning. Maybe it would have protected her against the sensations spreading down her arm.

"I'm Jack Montrose. And you are?"

He held out his hand. Lauren reached down and shook it. His nails were neat and clean. Everything about him was appealing. He held her hand for the required three pumps and then dropped it.

So this was her boss's playboy brother. The guy who never stayed with a woman longer than six months. He'd been profiled in *Detroit* magazine last year as one of the city's most eligible and elusive bachelors. Somehow he wasn't what Lauren had expected. "Lauren Belchoir."

"A DJ?" he asked.

Obviously he wasn't a fan. Sometimes she was afraid the only people who listened to her show were the insomniacs and the third-shift workers from the auto plant. "Yes, I'm Miss Lonely Hearts. I do the midnight-to-four shift."

At least, she used to. How was she going to ask this guy to be part of the Mile of Men?

He tilted his head to the side and studied her for a minute. Lauren reached up to tuck a strand of her unruly curly hair behind her ear. Her brother always teased her mercilessly about her hair's uncanny resemblance to Medusa's. Unfortunately she'd never been able to turn Duke or any other man into a stone.

"I bet you break a lot of hearts with that voice of yours," he said.

"What voice?" she asked. She knew guys liked her curves. She had the kind of hourglass figure that had been immensely popular fifty years ago, with full breasts, a tiny waist and full hips. But no man had ever noticed her voice.

"That soft, sexy one. You have a bedroom voice," he said, his own dropping an octave. His words sounded like a line. Which they probably were, considering his reputation. Disappointed in a way she didn't want to admit to, she pulled her hand free.

Taking a step backward, she put a good amount of distance between them. What kind of a thing was that to say to a woman?

"Don't get creeped out. I'm not coming on to you." He ran his hand through his thick hair and tipped his head to the side, studying her. He had a square jaw and laugh or sun lines around his eyes. His skin was tan even though it was winter. Lauren didn't think he was hitting a tanning bed, which meant he had to be spending some serious time outside. Maybe cross-country skiing?

"It sure sounded that way." At work she was kind of asexual. Most of the men here treated her like a kid sister or just one of the guys. The radio world was insular, safe. And Lauren was reminded once again that this man wasn't part of her world. And she didn't want to be attracted to Mr. Love 'Em and Leave 'Em.

"I was giving you a compliment," he said, shaking his head.

"Men aren't supposed to say stuff like that in the workplace."

He shook his head. "This is what's happened to society with all that damned political correctness. Men are programmed to notice women and to be attracted to them."

"That's a given."

"So we agree," he said, arching one eyebrow.

"To what?"

"That I was acting true to form."

She laughed. She couldn't help it. He was charming, and she wanted to stand in the hall all morning and enjoy sparring with him. And she had no doubt they'd be sparring.

"Don't even try to pretend you were just being nice. You were caressing my hand."

"So I like pretty women."

"I could tell. I'm not interested in being part of your flock."

He threw his head back and laughed. Lauren had to smile. Too many men took themselves too seriously. "Well, nice meeting you, Mr. Montrose."

"The pleasure was all mine, Lauren."

She walked away without looking back. She didn't care what the new guy said, she was keeping her distance from Mr. Jack Montrose. He was just the kind of man she'd have gone after. And that meant only one thing—he wasn't the right one for her.

Jack watched Lauren's swaying walk until she disappeared around the corner. He felt the old familiar stirring—that longing for something more. Normally he felt little more than light affection and lust for the women he dated. But Lauren had brought something hungry to life in the depths of his soul.

The part that he'd buried since his brief marriage had ended more than fifteen years ago.

Lauren Belchoir wasn't what he'd expected her to be. His brother had been singing her praises since he'd hired her two years ago. But Ty had a fatal weakness, and it was women. All women. He was the kind of man who loved hard and fast, burning a swath through single women in a blazing flame that reminded Jack of their father's life.

Their dad, Diamond Dave, had lived fast and furious, riding his motorcycle and performing daring stunts, challenging Evel Knievel for supremacy in bravery and courage. Unfortunately fate had caught up with Diamond Dave, leaving him paralyzed from the waist down after a stunt. That had changed the dynamic in Jack and Ty's parents' marriage and they'd never been the same.

But Jack had written off Ty's affection for Lauren Belchoir as a crush. God knew his brother had enough of them. Like their father's daring, Ty's approach to relationships was more likely to cause him to crash and burn than discover real love.

Lauren was Jack's fantasy woman—but he'd had his share of sex trophies over the years. Lauren was curvy and stacked, but her smile was sweet and her eyes gleamed with both humor and intelligence. And that was what really drew him. She had an unconscious grace when she moved that said she was at ease in her body.

Though he'd been on his way out of the building, he went back down the hall. Ty was coming off the executive elevator as Jack approached. With him were a man with thinning hair and about twenty extra pounds and a tall, thin woman with white-blond hair and an inner radiance.

"Hey, big bro, come and meet the team that's going to save us in the ratings." Ty was only an inch shorter than Jack's own six-foot frame. Unlike Jack's dark coloring, which came from their father, Ty had sandy blond hair and resembled their mother.

"Jack Montrose, meet Ray King and his producer, Didi Sera."

"It's a pleasure," Jack said, shaking their hands. "Where are you two from?"

"New Orleans."

"Orlando."

They both spoke at the same time.

"Which is it?" Jack asked. The Orlando market was much more prestigious than New Orleans.

"Both actually," Ray said with a shrug of his shoulders. "First Orlando, then more recently the Big Easy."

"Are you a DJ, Jack?" Didi asked.

"No. I own a record label and dabble in other business interests." He'd always preferred living out of the public spotlight. He'd grown up surrounded by his father's notoriety and that had been enough to convince Jack that the quiet life was for him.

"Speed Demon Records is one of the more successful indies," Ty said. Ty had always looked up to Jack. And Jack had felt the burden of being both older brother and father figure to Ty, because their own father had been too busy proving he hadn't lost his manhood when he'd lost the ability to walk.

"Single?" Ray asked.

Ty glanced at Ray but didn't say anything.

"Yes."

"Did you speak to Lauren?"

"Yes," Jack said.

"So are you going to do it?"

"Do what?"

"Nothing," Ray said, when Didi nudged him.

Jack looked at Ty. "I need to speak to you privately for a moment."

Ty nodded and turned to Ray and Didi. "I'll be up in a minute and we can finish going over the details."

Didi and Ray left the hall. Jack waited until the door closed behind them before he turned to his brother. "I want to know more about Lauren Belchoir."

"Why? You said you'd heard enough about her."

Jack wished they were twelve and nine again so he could get Ty into a headlock and force the answers he wanted out of his brother without having to answer a bunch of questions. But those days were gone, and Jack firmly reminded himself that mature men didn't have to beat up their younger brothers to get answers. "I ran into her."

Ty rubbed his chin. Jack knew he should never have brought up the subject. But the summer scent of her hair lingered with each breath he took and the remembered feel of her hand in his still made his palm tingle.

"She's a good worker, never late, hardly ever calls in sick. She bakes cookies for holidays and will work overtime without complaining." An unholy mirth shone from Ty's eyes.

"I'm not thinking about hiring her. Tell me some personal stuff."

"I thought you were dating some blonde. Besides, I have work to do."

"Ty…"

"Okay, but she's out of your league. She comes from a real traditional family—not like the how-many-marriages-can-I-have one like ours. Her mom is Evelina Belchoir. She has a syndicated television talk show for couples."

He'd heard of her mom. Which said a lot, because Jack didn't watch television. But Moira, his secretary, took her lunch break every day at one o'clock so she wouldn't miss a minute of Evelina's advice.

Jack and Ty's mom had been the stay-at-home, cookies-after-school type, but she'd kept marrying, trying to find something…Jack still didn't know what. She was motherly and doting and she'd move the world for her boys. But she'd never had good re-lationship skills.

"Does Lauren date?" Jack asked. He wanted to know everything about her. God, what did that say about him? Why did he have a hunger for her when they'd only just met? He had no answers.

"Funny you should ask. She's got her listeners searching for Mr. Right. In fact, the idea for this Mile of Men promotion came from her show. You should tune in to her show tonight," Ty said with that sly grin of his.

Jack shrugged. Ty said goodbye and went into his meeting. Jack walked out to his car on the snowy February Tuesday. He didn't know what to make of Lauren, but he knew he wasn't going to let her be.

Two

Lauren wasn't sure she liked the idea of being on in the morning, when more listeners would be tuning in. But the matter was out of her hands.

She adjusted her headphones as the last notes of Marvin Gaye's "Sexual Healing" played. The song had long been a favorite of hers, but tonight it had been requested by one of her listeners who'd gotten off work early and was heading home to his wife. Three o'clock was a weird time of night. Usually she took callers and just talked out her own problems.

God, she was a mess. Because tonight the only thing she'd been able to think about was Jack Montrose. She'd found a picture of him in *Radio and*

Records magazine. The issue was a few months old and had been playing up the fact that he'd taken a passion for doing what he loved and made it into a profitable venture. Speed Demon Records produced only new artists who created music in the spirit of old Motown classics from the forties and fifties.

"That was Marvin Gaye for Larry, heading home to his wife. If you're just tuning in, I'll be moving to the morning drive show starting next week. And I'm still searching for Mr. Right.

"I'm taking callers tonight to be signed up for WCPD's first annual Mile of Men. We're looking for Detroit's sexiest men to line Woodward Avenue starting at the Fox Theatre. Eligible women will then drive by and select a man by the number on his chest. They'll spend the day together and then everyone will be treated to a party at the Hilton downtown.

"Complete rules are available on our Web site. Listeners, you know I've been searching for Mr. Right, so help me find one to choose from for the station's big event."

Lauren pushed the button for the commercial break and looked over at the panel phones that were flashing with callers. Rodney, her producer, was answering the calls that came in and sending her a queue on her computer screen. She'd worked with Rodney for the last three years, and they had a good rhythm. Lauren read the caller names. Jack on line two made her pause. *Jack Montrose?*

Then she chided herself. It was three o'clock in the morning. Surely someone like Jack Montrose had other things to do than listen to her show.

She still had a minute-thirty until the commercial break was over. She pushed line two. "Hello, caller."

"Lauren?" he asked. His voice brushed over her like the remembered warmth of a summer's day.

She took a quick inward breath. It was him. She had no idea what to say. She almost dropped the call. But she'd never been cowardly with anyone and she wasn't about to start behaving that way now. "Jack Montrose."

"Am I on the air?" he asked.

Though she probably would have been smarter to wait until they were on the air, she hadn't. "No."

"Good. I'm not much on being in the public eye."

"I thought you didn't listen to my show."

"Once I met you, I had to give it a listen." Amusement laced his words. He sounded relaxed and almost lazy.

She pictured him sitting in front of a warm fire in a luxuriously appointed den, with a brandy snifter in his hand. The fire would flicker over his skin, which would be warm to the touch. In her mind, she put herself in the room with him. Settled next to him on an overstuffed couch. But those kinds of dreams were dangerous.

No one knew that better than her. She'd been loved and left many times. Bob was only the most recent.

The men who turned her on were always all wrong for her.

"What do you think of the show?" she asked. She didn't need his approval. But she wanted him to like what she did. This was a big part of who she was. More than a job, it was a calling, and she liked the dark hours after midnight.

"That I was right about your voice. You've been driving me out of my mind all night. Between that and those seductive songs you play." There was something alluring in his voice.

It didn't help matters that she'd spent the entire evening thinking of him as the slow, sensual songs played out. She remembered his hand on her shoulder. His touch burning through the thin layer of her clothing. What would it be like to have him caress her bare skin?

She shivered. Damn it. She was at work. Rodney rapped on the glass separating them and gestured to the clock. Forty-five seconds remained on the break.

"They were all requests. Do you have one? Is that why you called?"

"No. I called to talk to you. To have you to myself for a few minutes."

She couldn't respond to that. It was as if somehow he'd glimpsed a part of her she'd always hidden. She wanted to be some man's late-night fantasy. Not like Bob, who'd dumped her at midnight, saying that she was too independent and made him feel like a wimp.

"I've got to get back to work."

"Can I meet you for coffee when you're done with your shift?"

"Why?" she asked. God, she was running out of time. And she didn't know if she was happy about it. Be happy, she warned herself. This man has danger written all over him. Not physical jeopardy but the more chancy kind that would leave scars on her already battered heart.

"I want to get to know you better, Lauren."

She closed her eyes. She should just hang up. But she couldn't. She wanted to get to know him better, as well. Wanted for the first time in her life to be wrong about a guy. But this wasn't just about her. Ray thought Jack was perfect for the Mile of Men. "Give Rodney your number and I'll call you back."

Jack sank deeper into the leather seat of his Jaguar and let the sensuous sounds of Lauren's voice play over him. He sat in the nearly deserted parking lot of WCPD. Lauren had agreed to a quick cup of coffee, and he didn't question the reasons why getting to know this one woman was so important to him. He only knew that he had to see her again.

In the long hours since their morning encounter he'd been plagued by the memory of her shoulder under his palm, her fingers brushing his and the surety that her lips would be soft under his.

He'd called the woman he'd been seeing and told

her he couldn't see her anymore. She'd been disappointed but not overly so. The fact that their relationship had ended after only four months didn't really bother either of them. It had been…satisfying while it lasted.

But he knew he wasn't going to rest easy until he'd unraveled the mystery of Lauren. Was this what his father felt each time he met a new woman? Or was this the thing that eluded both of his parents, that kept them searching?

He heard her sign off and turned off his car. He climbed out of the vehicle and headed toward the entrance of the building.

He could have called Ty and asked him for the security code to unlock the lobby doors, but Jack was reluctant to give his brother any more fodder. Instead he stood in the cold Detroit night, huddling deeper into his wool overcoat and waiting for a woman who could be the beginning of a new six-month chapter in his life.

When he'd turned sixteen, Jack had realized that his life seemed to move in six-month cycles. Friends, his mother's boyfriends, father's girlfriends, sports— all seemed to last only that long. He'd tested his theory a couple of times and it had proved true. His own interest in new things lasted no more than six months. The only enduring interest he'd found was his love of music.

Women, music, cars, houses. He surrounded himself with whatever was fashionable and pleasurable at the moment and felt no qualms when it was time to move on. It was an inescapable part of his nature, and he'd come to terms with it.

The door opened and he stepped forward. For a minute he couldn't breathe. Her thick black hair curled around her heart-shaped face. She tilted her head to the side, studying him in the harsh glow of the security lamp.

"Hello, Jack."

Her voice was even more potent in person, brushing over his senses and starting a tingling at the base of his spine. He wanted to feel those full lips of hers against his skin while she spoke.

"Lauren," he said. Oh, yeah, he was a smooth talker.

"You want to follow me to the diner I mentioned on the phone?" She pulled a pair of leather gloves from her pocket and put them on.

"I'll drive us."

He cupped her elbow and led her across the parking lot to his car. He knew she didn't need his assistance to walk across the pavement, but he had been unable to wait another second to touch her. Even in such an avuncular way.

Rationally he knew he couldn't feel the softness of her skin through the layers of coat and gloves. But with the sweet floral scent of her perfume filling his nostrils, he imagined he could. Damn, he wished it was summer and she was wearing something that bared her arms.

"You were listening to my show," she said.

"Yes." He reached out and flicked off the radio. He backed out of the parking lot and headed for the diner she'd mentioned. "Interesting show. Tell me about your listeners fixing you up."

"Oh, that. Well, I kind of have a horrible track record with men. The latest and greatest being my fiancé, Bob, who dumped me on New Year's Eve at a huge party that my parents threw for us. We were supposed to announce our engagement that night."

"Ouch."

She gave him a half smile. "Yeah. But one thing I realized after I got over the anger and the embarrassment was that I didn't really miss Bob. Which made me start thinking about the men I seemed to be drawn to. I decided to take a page from my mom's book."

"Which is?"

"Throw the problem out to the listeners and see what they come up with. My mom's a TV talk-show host."

"I know. My secretary is a huge fan."

"Not you?"

"No. I solve my own problems."

"Big macho man."

He chuckled. She made him feel good deep inside. He liked that she wasn't intimidated by who he was. "Yeah, that's me."

"So what's your usual problem-solving method?" she asked. Her tone was softer than a moment before, and he realized that she was doing the same thing he was—feeling him out and searching for answers about the person behind the spark that had flashed between them.

"What do you think?" he asked. He braked to a stop for a red light and glanced at her. Her features looked delicate in the half light that filled the car. She seemed like something ethereal that might slip away. A kind of sexy pixie that had happened into his car by accident and could disappear at any second.

"Something involving a club," she said, waggling her eyebrows at him.

The light changed and he eased forward. "Nice, Belchoir. Really nice. But you're not quite on the mark. I'm not the violent type."

She bit her lower lip, and for a moment his foot slipped off the gas pedal. Her lips were luscious and he wanted to feel them under his own.

"Yeah, but you're not passive either."

"Certainly not around you."

"What's that mean?" she asked.

"Just that I don't normally leave my home in the middle of the night to have coffee with a woman."

"Should I feel flattered?"

"Don't get sassy."

"Sorry. I'm just afraid."

"Of me?"

"I guess. There's something about you, Jack Montrose, that makes me wish…"

"What?"

"For something experience has taught me doesn't exist."

He didn't want to know what that thing was. There was a sadness in her voice and in her eyes that made him want to pull her into his arms and promise her he'd never let her feel that way again. And he knew that he wasn't the kind of man who could really make promises like that. Dammit. He knew then that this coffee thing was a mistake, and one he wouldn't repeat. Because Lauren wasn't like the women he'd dated in the past. She wasn't going to be satisfied with only six months, and for the first time in his life he wondered if he would be.

Lauren ordered a chai, and Jack ordered regular coffee and added a little cream to it. An awkward silence filled the space between them. She didn't know what to say to him. They'd only just met and yet she felt as if she'd known him forever.

Lauren toyed with her spoon until Jack reached across the table and covered her hand with his. His hand was big and warm. His nails were buffed and square—nicer looking than hers, because despite her mother's lectures, Lauren still bit them. She was a little embarrassed and thought she should pull her hand away.

"Nervous?" he asked.

His voice seemed even deeper in the early morning hour. He wore an Icelandic cable-knit sweater and a pair of jeans so faded and soft that they clung to his thighs. She wished she'd slid in beside him on the bench seat in the booth instead of playing it safe. She wanted to be cuddled next to his big frame. To lean against his shoulder and just listen to him talk.

"No. You're just a guy and I already got your number."

He rubbed his thumb over her knuckles before stroking the center of her palm. Little tingles of awareness spread upward, making her shift restlessly on the bench.

"Just a guy. That's harsh. How many guys have picked you up after work and taken you to a classy joint like this one for coffee?"

Lauren glanced around the diner. It had character. The chrome-and-Formica tables and vinyl-padded seats were never going to grace the pages of any style magazine. But she liked it. "This place isn't that bad."

"What about the guy?"

She shifted her hand in his grip and held his large one in hers, palm up. She traced the lines on his palm with her free hand, keeping her gaze firmly away from Jack's stormy one that seemed to see too much.

"Lauren?"

"The guy's not bad either." She dropped his hand and wrapped both of hers around her hot teacup to rid herself of all connection to Jack. He was disturbing to her on too many levels.

"What's the problem then?"

God, she was a mess. She should have gone on her mother's show. "Girls Who Can't Trust Their Own Instincts." It would probably be a ratings boon, and people across the country would give advice on why she shouldn't be sitting in this booth with Jack Montrose.

"It's just…this is odd. Why did you call me tonight?"

"I want to get to know you better."

"How much better?"

"Naked," he said, lifting one eyebrow and gazing straight through her to her soul.

She wanted to see him naked, too. He probably had an all-over tan, and she could tell from the cut of his sweater and jeans that there wasn't any spare fat on his body. "Well, that's to the point."

He leaned across the table, all possessive male intent on keeping the advantage. Another shiver slithered down her spine and she leaned toward him. Their faces were inches apart. She felt the brush of his breath against her cheek.

"You were hedging toward it too slowly for my tastes."

"I'm not a speedy person."

"I am."

His gaze fastened on her mouth. She licked her

lips and heard him groan. "Then you should try out our Mile of Men."

"No, thanks."

"Why not?"

"Because I don't want a strange woman picking me off the line. I want you."

"Why?"

He shrugged. "Who knows? Tell me about you, Lauren. What do I make you wish for?"

She sank back against the chair and took a sip of her tea. "I thought you'd forgotten that."

"I forget nothing."

"Really?"

"Truly. Photographic memory. It's a pain in the neck sometimes."

"Like me?" she asked. Anything to avoid discussing her ill-timed remark earlier. What had she been thinking?

"I wouldn't say that."

"Nah, but you'd think it." She should finish her tea, say thank you and get the hell out of here before she said anything else she'd regret revealing to him.

"Not about you. Tell me."

"Do we know each other well enough to exchange secrets?" she asked, stalling.

"I want to see you naked, so I think we have to swap secrets."

"No quickie one-night thing?"

"Would you be happy with that?" he asked.

She thought about it. A one-night stand wasn't her thing, but Jack teased at something deep inside her that she was afraid to let out. Something oddly vulnerable that all the men who'd loved and left her had damaged, and she didn't want to risk that again. And a one-night stand—well, that was about lust, not about emotions and scarred souls.

"Lauren?"

"No. I want more than that with you."

He lifted her hand from the table and brushed his lips over the back of her hand. "I knew it. Trust me."

She tugged but he wouldn't release her hand. Finally she realized that he wasn't going to do anything he didn't want to do, anything that wasn't in his plans. It had been a long time since she'd met a man who didn't let her set the pace and make all the decisions.

"It seems silly."

He said nothing, only waited.

She dropped her head and looked at the chipped Formica table. "I wish I still believed that Prince Charming was out there, because you have the trappings of being one."

"A fairy-tale prince, eh?"

She glanced up. He was studying her as if he'd never seen her before. "Don't let the tough-girl act fool you. Deep inside I want the white picket fence, like every other woman. It's just that I've spent the last ten years kissing toads."

"So experience tells you that even though I look like I could be the prince, I'm the toad?"

"You got it."

"What would it take to prove you wrong?"

"A lot of trust, a little love and…the man of my dreams."

"That's a tall order," he said. "How about a lot of fun, a little daring and me?"

Three

Jack knew he was no fairy-tale prince. In fact, given his lifestyle, he was probably more like the toads Lauren had kissed. But he didn't want to let this thing go so easily.

The diner was quiet in this early-morning hour. A few people trickled in and he noted their factory uniforms. They probably worked the early shift. Two guys waved at Lauren and she smiled back at them.

"Longtime listeners. They set me up with their crew chief, Joe Brigg. We're getting him to participate in the Mile of Men."

He felt a surge of jealousy that he knew was irrational. "Are you still seeing this Joe?"

"Nah, he wanted a traditional sort of wife. And despite the fact that I'm low-key, I'm not stay-at-home material. I love my show and my listeners. Giving that up would be hard."

Jack didn't know what to say to that. His life was all about change. He didn't know from one day to the next what might strike his fancy. He ran a record label, true, but he had enough leeway in that job to take off at a moment's notice.

"Boy, do I know how to end a conversation or what?" she asked lightly, but there was more than a little unease in her posture.

He reached for her hand where it lay on the table. He held it loosely in his own grip. Her fingers were cold, and he stroked his thumb over her knuckles, trying to warm her a little. He wanted to pull her out of the bench seat and around to his side of the table.

Wanted to tuck her up against his chest and promise her that the days of kissing toads were gone. But he wasn't the right kind of guy to make that kind of promise. The one time he'd tried to make something last longer than six months had backfired on him and the woman he'd made promises to.

"I asked for the truth," he said at last. He prized himself on honesty in all relationships. In fact, he'd ruined two friendships because of his fanatic devotion to the facts.

Lauren was watching him carefully, seeming to measure the man he was. Jack had never been so conscious of the fact that he might not measure up to whatever standards she had that said "man."

She gave him a sad-looking smile. "You did. Should I have lied?"

It would have been easier on him. He could have blithely continued with his seduction plan. A nice, easy affair that would have been mutually satisfying. At the end of it they could've gone their own ways with no hard feelings. Just pleasant memories. "No. I don't want there to be lies between us."

"Still want to get naked with me?" she asked in that husky alto voice of hers.

God, he'd give five years off his life to have her naked in bed and just listen to that voice talking dirty to him. "Hell, yes."

"Wish you'd kept it light?" she asked, tilting her head to the side.

Now it was his turn to be honest, and for the first time in his life he didn't want to be. Because the truth would put a barrier between them. And he wanted to be breaking down the problems between them instead of reinforcing them. "Yes and no."

"Why no?"

"Things were uncomplicated before. You were just an attractive woman. Now you're…"

"What?" she asked. Her eyes met his steadily, and he felt a pressure to not disappoint this woman.

"More." It was all he could say. He wasn't going to tell her that she set a fire in him that had nothing to do with lust and everything to do with the longing he carried inside since childhood. A longing for something intangible that he'd always known was missing from his life.

"Well, that's one thing in our favor."

"It's everything."

She took another sip of her tea and played with the ring on her finger. Her nails were bitten to the quick and not exactly glamorous, but he liked the little flaw. The ring was some sort of Celtic knot made out of sterling. He skimmed his gaze over her, studying her. Noticing the funky earrings buried in her thick hair and the simple gold chain that disappeared under the collar of her maroon sweater.

"I guess we should be going," she said. A tendril of her hair curled around her cheekbone.

He reached up and brushed it back, tucking the curl behind her ear. Her hair was soft—softer than anything he'd ever touched before. He rubbed a strand of hair between his forefinger and thumb.

Lauren sat still, watching him with those wide brown eyes of hers and making him want…her. *Just her.* He tugged on the strand of hair and she leaned toward him. He leaned closer. So close, he felt the brush of her breath against his mouth with each exhalation.

He caressed her face. Her skin was soft and he traced a light pattern over her high cheekbones down to those full lips of hers that had been driving him out of his mind. He stroked her lower lip with his thumb. She caught her breath.

He knew then that whatever was between them, it was too late to keep it light. Physically there was more than a spark that bespoke of mutual attraction. His gut said this woman matched him passion for passion. And he freely admitted he wanted to explore that.

But not at a price that Lauren would find too high to pay. And not at a price that he'd regret asking her for. And certainly not at a price that would rock the solid world he'd built for himself.

Lauren studied Jack as he drove back to her car. He was like no other man she'd ever met, and her throat tightened at the thought of never getting to explore the magic that had blossomed between them. Why couldn't they?

He brought to life more of her senses than any other man she'd ever met. He made her laugh and think. And challenged her with his acerbic wit. He was the kind of man she'd always dreamed of finding, and only now did she understand that she'd been settling for the mirage, the illusion of the real thing, never realizing that it could be solid.

Jack was certainly solid, she thought with a grin. But she needed more than the physical. That article she'd read about him bothered her. However, because her mom had lived in the spotlight most of Lauren's life, she knew that interviews didn't always give the reader all the facts.

"I read an article about you in *Detroit* magazine," she said once they were headed back to the station. Jack had put on a Paul Simon CD, one from the late eighties that had the mellow influences of Africa in it.

"Did you?" he asked with a wry grin. -

She toyed with letting him keep her away from what she wanted to know. But in the end, the heavy beating of her heart and the warnings in her mind convinced her otherwise. "Don't be coy. I want to know if the article was true."

He sighed and fiddled with the volume on the stereo but didn't turn to look at her even when he had to stop for a traffic light. "I don't think of myself as the most eligible bachelor in the city, if that's what you're asking."

Let it go. But she couldn't. "I'm not. I want to know about the six-month thing."

"Sweetheart, we just met."

She knew what he was saying. Her rational mind said they were still essentially strangers, but she'd shared her heart and the secret she'd always longed to find in a mate with him.

And now she needed to know if the guy that she'd started liking the minute they'd met was going to break her heart. Should she let him in or keep him at the safe arm's length that she'd kept all other men? And with Jack, would that be easy to do?

"I know, but I told you a secret. And that article made it sound like you had a phobia about things lasting longer than that."

"Well, I do," he said, his voice even deeper than its normal tonality.

"Why?" she asked. She'd grown up with one of the country's leading relationship experts, so Lauren knew firsthand that you had to keep hammering away at the same question until you found the real answer.

"It's just been my experience. I'm forty-five. I know a lot about myself and my habits."

"And you can't teach an old dog new tricks?" she asked around the tightness in her throat. *Forty-five.* She probably had sounded like a child to him. Saying that she still wanted happily ever after. Her gut argued that she hadn't. That the truth she'd seen shining in Jack's eyes was the same desire as hers.

"Watch who you're calling an old dog," he said lightly.

She watched the streetlights out the window and tried to pretend it didn't matter. That his superficial answer to her very real question didn't hurt. Why should it? She'd just met him. Though it felt different in her soul.

"Lauren…"

She didn't look at him. Didn't want to right now. Paul Simon played quietly in the background, and Lauren closed her eyes and concentrated on the lyrics of the song instead of the man who perplexed her and made her yearn for a deeper connection with him.

He cursed under his breath. She felt the car slow and then stop. She opened her eyes. He'd pulled onto the shoulder. She shifted her head on the back of the seat to watch him.

"Why are you stopping?" she asked. His features were stark with only the dashboard illumination. He scarcely resembled the stylish man that she knew him to be. And she wondered if this was the real Jack Montrose seated next to her in the dark. When all the trappings of looks fell away, all that was left was the heart of who he was.

"Because I can't chase you when I'm driving," he said.

"I don't understand."

He twisted to face her, cupping her jaw in both of his hands. It was the third time he'd touched her face, and she couldn't help the elemental awareness that shot through her.

"Let me explain it. I'm sorry I can't promise you more than six months. That I can't say that you're the one woman who will make me want more than any other one has. But it's just too soon."

"Hey, you were the one who said you wanted to get to know me naked."

"I still do. But naked doesn't mean lasting."

"I know," she said softly.

Jack tugged her into his arms. He held her loosely

but securely. She relaxed and let go of the hurt that had been building in the pit of her stomach. He smelled like fresh pine, and she burrowed closer to his warmth, inhaling deeply.

"You confuse me," he said, rubbing his chin against the top of her head.

"I'm just a woman."

"And therein lies the mystery." She tipped her head back and their eyes met. "I can't make any promises. But dammit, woman, I can't let this go either."

"Me, too."

She lifted up and met his mouth as it descended on hers. His lips brushed softly over hers, keeping the embrace light until her mouth tingled and she ached to know his taste. She opened her mouth, but he lifted his lips and dropped kisses down the column of her neck.

She lifted her hands, plunging them into his thick hair and lifting his head, bringing his mouth back to hers. She opened her lips against his. Breathed in his breath and gave him back hers. Then she skimmed her tongue over the seam of his lips and pushed it inside, tasting him as deeply as she could.

Something long hidden inside her heart sprang to life, and as the timbre of the embrace changed and Jack took control of it, she acknowledged that maybe six months with Jack wouldn't be so bad. Because she knew she'd always regret it if she let him leave her life after just one night.

* * *

Lauren tasted as he knew she would. Like sunshine and vitality and a hint of spiciness. He'd made love to many women over the course of his life, and for the first time he felt something beyond just lust. It intensified the arousal flowing through his veins.

He felt each exhalation of her breath like a brand on his skin. He felt each minute movement of her body as she undulated against him like a velvet glove tightening on his private flesh. He felt each sound she made all the way to his soul and he knew he'd never kiss a woman again without remembering Lauren.

He thrust his tongue deep inside, seeking more of her, needing to delve deeper and claim her completely as his own. Her skin felt soft under his touch, just as he'd known it would.

His mind shut down and he was guided by instinct. Slipping his hands down her back, rubbing the individual vertebrae of her spine, slipping underneath the loose sweater she wore.

Her skin was warm to the touch and she shivered as he stroked his hand lazily under and down. She moaned deep in her throat, and the sound went straight to his groin, hardening him even more.

He shifted on the seat, pulling her more fully against him. Her breasts nestled into the hard planes of his chest. He reached for the hem of her sweater, starting to raise it, when he remembered where they were.

In a parked car on the side of the road. He was a

respected businessman, not a horny teenager alone with his first girl. He pulled his hands away from her flesh with a lingering caress. He lifted his mouth from hers, but her lips were full, swollen from his kisses, and he couldn't resist one more round before he lifted her off his lap and set her in the passenger seat.

He drew in several deep breaths, finding some control before he looked at Lauren. Her arms were wrapped around her waist and her eyes were closed.

"That almost got out of hand," he said. Because he couldn't say what he really wanted to, which was, *To hell with getting your car, let's go back to my place and explore every nuance of the attraction between us.*

But Lauren wasn't his usual kind of woman, and he'd heard more than the words she'd said in the diner. She wanted a man who would court her. A man who looked behind that made-for-sin body to the woman underneath. And by damned if he wasn't going to try to be that man.

He didn't understand why. Didn't even care to explain it, because he knew that if he tried, he'd realize that failure loomed in front of him. He'd never been good at the long haul, but holding Lauren in his arms had made him realize he had to at least try. At least make the effort of being the kind of man she wanted. Because he wanted to be her man.

"Yeah, thanks for stopping it."

She didn't sound that grateful. In fact, she

sounded mad. He realized the way she was holding her body wasn't for warmth but for some sort of comfort.

He'd never freaking understand women. "I was being a gentleman."

She lifted both eyebrows at him. "And I said thanks."

"Lauren?" He grabbed onto his temper with both hands. He was still violently aroused and wanted nothing more than to say the hell with this behavior that was foreign to him. Did she want a red-hot affair that lasted no more than a week? "In order to find Prince Charming you have to actually recognize him when he rides up to the castle—and then you have to let him in."

She bit her lower lip, which was still red and swollen from his kisses. "Are you saying maybe I deserved to kiss those toads?"

He wished at least one of them were a little confident here. At least one of them knew where they were going, had some experience in this out-of-control feeling. Was this what his dad had experienced each time he'd launched his motorcycle into the air? If so, Jack wondered how he'd gotten used to it.

Lauren was staring at him and he realized he hadn't responded to her. "No. I'm saying that maybe you've forgotten what to do when Mr. Right rides up."

"And you're Mr. Right?"

"I'm not Mr. Wrong," he said. He knew that with a surety that came from deep inside him. He might not like what she made him feel, but no way was he going to ease out of her life.

He put the car back in gear and pulled back onto the road. They arrived at the parking lot and Lauren had her seat belt off and her hand on the door before he even shut the car off. He grabbed her arm to stop her from leaping out of the vehicle.

"What's the hurry?" he asked.

"No hurry. I just…I need to get home."

"I'm sorry, Lauren," he said. And meant it. He had the feeling that he'd hurt her and had no idea how.

"Don't be. You were definitely a gentleman and I enjoyed our coffee and conversation."

"But?"

She shrugged. "You were right. I do have barriers that I keep between myself and the rest of the world. And I'm not sure I can let you inside."

"This is new to me, too. Normally I'd have taken you home with me."

"Why didn't you?"

"Because you're different than every other woman and…"

"And?" she asked.

She seemed poised on the edge of running, and he knew he didn't have the words to make her stay.

"And that scares me."

She smiled then and he knew he'd blundered into

the right thing to say. And hoped he could keep on doing it, because being with Lauren was like riding ninety miles an hour down a twisting mountain road on his motorcycle.

Four

The peal of the doorbell pulled her from an erotic dream. At first she didn't want to leave the bed. Tried to cling to the images in her head and the feeling of Jack's strong body over hers. But the ringing was insistent and her dream lover faded away.

She pushed to her feet, grabbing her tattered quilted robe and shrugging into it. The robe had been a gift from her maternal grandmother, Grandma Jean, when she'd graduated from college. Since Grandma Jean had died six months later, the robe was now Lauren's way of experiencing a hug from her grandmother.

The doorbell rang again and she hurried to answer it. She checked the security peephole. A delivery man, but not her usual guy. Her mother was constantly sending books, videos and homemade cookies via FedEx to her.

For some reason, even though she was thirty, her mom insisted on treating her as if she were twelve.

"Miss Belchoir?"

"Yes," she said.

"These are for you."

He handed her a flower bouquet in a heavy vase. Lauren stared at him for a minute, not really sure what to say. Who had sent her flowers?

He turned to go.

"Wait. Let me get you—"

"Everything's been taken care of. Have a nice day."

Lauren eased back inside her house and shut the door with her foot. The bouquet wasn't something as common as roses or gerbera daisies. It was orchids and stargazer lilies and…damn, a bunch of blooms that she didn't know the name of.

She took the cut-glass vase into her kitchen and set it on the table. The card was there, in an envelope with her name on the outside. There was a computer printout on the back of the envelope, but her first name had been handwritten in a strong masculine scrawl.

She told herself she was wrong, that Jack wouldn't have sent her flowers. By even entertaining the thought, she was setting herself up for disappointment. She opened the tab of the envelope with her fingernail and pulled that card out.

Thanks for last night. Will you have dinner with me?
Jack

She dropped the card and leaned forward on the table, resting her head on her folded arms. Was she really going to do this? Was she really going to go out with a man who made her feel…too many things? A man who was mercurial and changed with the wind?

She stood up and grabbed the phone before she realized she didn't have his number. Instead she dialed the station and asked for Ty.

"Montrose," Ty said, answering on the first ring. She could tell he was in a good mood because there was laughter in his voice. But then, Ty seldom took anything, even the failing ratings of the station, too seriously.

"Ty, it's Lauren."

"Hey, what's up? Are you calling in sick?"

"What? No. I, uh, I need a phone number."

"Call the operator," he said with a laugh in his voice.

She'd always felt as if Ty was not only her boss but her friend. Since both of them had deplorable taste in the opposite sex, they had commiserated a time or two over margaritas about their pathetic ex-mates. What would he think when she asked about his brother? "I need Jack's number."

"He didn't give it to you?"

Maybe this hadn't been a good idea. "Are you trying to get on my bad side?"

"Hell, no." Ty rattled off his brother's numbers—home, office and cell phone.

"Did you give him mine?" she asked. Her address was unlisted because she'd had a problem with a stalker a few years ago.

"No. But he did call and ask me to have Pat give your address to the florist down the street."

She didn't know how she felt about that. It was the kind of thing she'd come to expect from Ty, her friend. "Should you have given me his number?"

He gave a big laugh. "I think my big brother can protect himself against you."

"Yeah, I think so," she said. "Thanks."

She disconnected the call with Ty and dialed Jack's office number before she could change her mind. While the phone rang she tried to think of what she'd say to the secretary or receptionist who answered.

"Montrose," Jack said. His voice was deep and dark—everything she remembered it being.

"Hello," she said. Her thoughts scattered. She'd been hoping for a few additional seconds to gather her wits while she was connected to him.

"Lauren. How are you?" he asked.

"Fine. Thanks for the flowers." With that kind of fast thinking it was hard to believe she made her living talking. She took a few deep breaths. She needed to calm down. He was just a guy. Just a guy.

"You're welcome. I told them late-afternoon delivery. Did they wake you up?"

"Yes, but it was time for me to get out of bed."

"Damn. Now I've got an image in my head of you all soft and cozy straight from bed."

"What kind of image is it?"

"The kind that a PC girl like you doesn't want to hear about."

"Rated R?"

"Only if I tone it down," he said.

Lauren laughed. She liked him. Liked his honesty about how he reacted to her and liked how he made her feel when she spoke to him. He was so much more than just a guy, she thought. She'd realized that from the moment he'd shown up after her show.

"About dinner," she said.

"If I apologize, will you say yes?"

"I was calling to accept. Don't apologize. I like your fantasies."

"You don't even know what they are," he said.

"I know they involve you and me."

"That's right. They do."

"Then that's all I need to know," she said quietly.

"How do you feel about the outdoors?" he asked.

"Um…I'm kind of a shopping-mall and coffee-bar girl."

"This will be painless and lots of fun."

"If it isn't you'll owe me one."

"One what?"

"Whatever I want, and it might be some sort of metrosexual spa date."

"Deal," he said.

"Are you that confident?" she asked.

"Hell, yeah!"

"When are we getting together—before or after my show?"

"After. I'll come by your place and take you to work so you don't have to worry about your car."

"Isn't that presumptuous?"

"No. I always pick my dates up and take them home whenever they're ready to leave," he said quietly.

She gave him her address and hung up the phone, aware that she'd started something with Jack that she was going to finish—no matter what it cost her emotionally.

Jack sat alone in his car once again, listening to Lauren. This was her last night on the midnight shift and her listeners were saying goodbye. It was a sweet evening that made him care about her even more. She really touched the lives of her listeners every day. And they were going to miss her.

Jack felt a pang of envy. He'd worked with a number of people over the years but never made the kind of connection that Lauren had with her listeners.

He'd learned a lot listening to her during the last four days. She seemed open and vulnerable and very intimate. He wanted that intimacy.

He heard her signature sign-off song, Stevie Ray Vaughan's "Shake for Me," and left the car. There was a lot of moisture in the air, and he knew snow was on the way.

It was cold outside, but Jack was hot enough to give off steam. And that had little to do with the heat from his car and cashmere coat. Lauren had whipped him into a frenzy. Every night while he listened to her in the dark he felt the tension growing. Felt the need—no, the craving—for her growing.

Felt his body desperately hungering for something he'd never wanted before—complete possession of a woman. Not just any woman either. Lauren Belchoir was the only one who would do.

Five minutes later Lauren walked out of the building and stopped. Her thick hair hung in soft waves past her shoulders, and he could tell from the way it was mussed that she'd been playing with it. He noticed her lips were shiny and glossy. She'd taken the time to primp before she'd come outside to meet him.

That got him in the gut. No matter that they both were not sure what was going on here. They both needed it. Both wanted it.

She stared directly up at him, and he felt a tightening in his gut that warned this was more than seduction. That hinted that maybe this woman might be more than a six-month cycle in a life made up of them. That promised a warmth Jack had never experienced yet always longed to.

"Hi," she said, her voice soft and sexy. Just for

his ears alone, no filter of the radio to blunt the appeal of it.

"Hey," he said, moving toward her because he couldn't help himself.

He wanted to feel her shoulders under his hands. Her body pulled flush to his and her mouth under his own. He wanted to plunder and leave no doubt in either of their minds who was in control here.

Because in his gut he knew he wasn't.

He pulled her closer to him until they were full-body chest to breast, groin to groin and breath mingling with breath. And only then did something inside him release. He hadn't realized how empty his arms had been without her until this moment.

She tipped her head to the side, staring up at him with those wide, honest eyes. "I guess you're happy to see me?"

"Hell, don't play innocent with me. You've been seducing me all night long with your bedroom voice and those songs that are made for hot sex." His body was rapidly hardening now that he had her in his arms. She rocked against his hard-on and he nearly moaned.

It would be so easy to make this all about sex. And he wanted it to only be about sex. But when she looked up at him, her eyes searching for something in his gaze, he knew that it was more. She was soft and feminine despite her independence and sassy attitude.

He started to drop his hands and move away but

she canted her hips toward him. Slid her hands around his neck and rose up on her tiptoes. "They were all requests."

He bent his head, rubbed his lips over hers. Tasted the spices of the tea blend she must have been drinking.

"I have a request."

She nipped at his bottom lip and then plunged her tongue into his mouth. He moved his hands into her hair, holding her head, tipping it back so that he was in control. He met her tongue with his, sliding it deep into the back of her mouth so that he could taste all of her. Know all of her. And conquer…all of her.

Despite the fact that he'd limited her range of motion, she didn't back down. She scraped her fingernail along the lower edge of his ear and then under the collar of his shirt.

She twisted her head to the side, running her tongue along the length of his jaw. "What was your request?"

"Your mouth on mine."

"Granted," she said with that half smile of hers.

Then she sank closer to him. Wrapped her arms around his waist and rested her head on the crook of his shoulder. "Thanks for picking me up."

He hugged her back, knowing it was cold and late and he was starting something that he really had no business starting with this woman at this time. She still believed in happily ever after. She still wanted some kind of girlish forever love, and he'd never believed in it.

All his life he'd seen lovers leaving, first in his parents' marriage and then in his own relationships. He'd never seen something that could last. Something that was good. Something that he freaking wanted as much as he wanted Lauren. And he wanted to keep her tucked up against him, her warm exhalations at the base of his throat and her curvy body pressed against his.

"Let's go. I think it's time I fulfilled some requests for you."

"Promise?"

The hint of vulnerability. The hesitation in her sweet voice made him pause. "Don't expect too much. I'm still wearing a toad's skin and I—"

She placed her fingers over his lips. "Just trying is enough for me. Where's your car?"

He led her to a bright yellow Hummer H2. Using the remote keyless entry he unlocked the doors. "This is mine. I picked it up this morning."

"Why?"

"I was tired of the Jag."

"Wasn't it new?" she asked.

He didn't understand why she was questioning him. Maybe she didn't like Hummers. But he needed something big and capable of off-roading. He had felt the need for a new vehicle. "Yeah, so?"

"Nothing," she said and climbed into the vehicle.

But he knew something had changed and he didn't know how to fix it.

Lauren loved the way Jack drove. It was a simple thing, but he maneuvered the car with an ease that made her realize he was always in control. "Did your dad teach you to drive?"

"Yeah. Do I make you nervous?"

"Absolutely not. You're a very good driver."

He said nothing until he braked at a stoplight. "My dad wasn't around a lot, but he did give me one piece of advice about driving."

"Is it something that only a Montrose can know? A Diamond Dave secret that's passed from one daredevil to the next?"

"Ha. I'm not an edge-of-the-seat crazy stuntman."

"I didn't think your dad was crazy. We went to see him twice when I was a kid. I almost stopped breathing when he made his motorcycle flip over."

Jack chuckled. The light changed and he started driving again with the same speed and skill, and she realized he hadn't really answered her question. Maybe he wasn't comfortable being the son of a celebrity.

God knew she hated being tracked down and questioned by her mom's rabid fans. "Sorry if I made you uncomfortable."

"How did you do that?" he asked, taking one hand from the wheel and putting it on her leg. His warmth burned through the fabric of her jeans. It was hot and heavy and made her aware—achingly aware—of how close his touch was to her center.

Suddenly she felt as if she should cross her legs. But doing so would announce her nervousness at his touch. Her thoughts were scattered and she didn't know if she could get them marshaled. What had they been talking about?

She glanced over at Jack when he squeezed her leg. In the fleeting light of the street lamps he went in and out of focus, much as he did in her mind. He was clear to her one second, deep-dark mysterious the next.

She'd been trying to find out about his past. His dad, Diamond Dave Montrose. Second only to Evel Knievel, the daring stuntman who'd jumped his motorcycle over anything.

"You okay? I asked you why you thought I was uncomfortable."

She shook herself. She needed to keep her wits about her. "Yeah, I'm fine. I worried that by asking about your dad I might have upset you. Ty talks about him all the time."

"Men don't get upset. That's a girlie thing."

"Having emotions doesn't make you girlie. Everyone has them."

"Right, but only woman have to dissect them and get…bothered by them."

"I forgot that you were a big, bad he-man. My mistake."

"Don't let it happen again," he said with a grin that made her melt. He was a grade-A flirt and tease. She knew without a doubt that if she kept things light between them they could have a red-hot affair that would burn out before summer.

He didn't even keep a car more than six months. Make that matter, she thought. But the thrill of being with him made the vehicle thing hard to ignore. It was another warning that this wasn't forever. That her goal of marriage someday soon wasn't going to happen with this man by her side.

She wanted more from him—already Jack meant something to her. She knew he didn't want to talk about his dad and she had no idea why. But she wasn't going to allow him to evade her. He was her break-the-rules guy. So that meant she wasn't going to politely do what he wanted. She was going to go for everything, risk everything.

"You're avoiding talking about your father."

He scratched a pattern in the fabric of her jeans, each stroke of his finger curving deeper toward her inner thigh, higher on her leg. She felt her body softening, preparing to welcome him inside.

"I'm not. I just don't want to spoil your image of Diamond Dave," he said.

Lauren took his hand in hers, tracing over his large knuckles and studying that strong hand. "Not a good dad?"

"Let's just say the spotlight was more important

than teaching two boys how to drive," Jack said, his deep voice husky. She knew he was telling her something he didn't want to.

"Did you teach Ty?" she asked. Duke had taught her, but only because he'd had to do community service for drinking at a football game and her father had negotiated her driving lessons as suitable time served.

"Yes. But just because he believed the crap our dad was feeding him and I didn't want Ty to end up in a wheelchair like Dave."

"What crap?" she asked, holding his hand in both of hers now. She wanted to give him some simple comfort in any way that she could. She knew that it was little, next to nothing, but this was all she had to offer.

"That life is best lived at ninety-five miles per hour. Flying high and living large. 'Don't slow down for anyone, boys. That's all you need to know to drive a car.'"

Her heart ached at the emptiness she heard in Jack's voice. He'd taken those words to heart. She didn't know what to say. Because she knew Jack would scoff if she even intimated that he needed comfort for his childhood. "Well, you did a great job of teaching yourself."

She wanted to change the subject but had no idea how to.

"Hell, I didn't, not really. I like that feeling that comes with flying. I like being out of control. And I made peace with that side of myself.

"How?"

"By believing that nothing lasts forever."

"Nothing?"

He lifted their joined hands and brushed his lips against hers. "Nothing, but some things make the fleetingness of life worthwhile."

"Me?"

"You," he said, his deep voice dropping an octave.

Five

Jack had learned early that he needed to spend a lot of time outdoors. Sports were the one constant in his ever-changing life. Exercise was something he enjoyed. Lauren eyed him curiously when he turned off the highway and pulled to a stop near a deserted park.

"What are we doing?" she asked.

"Snowshoeing. There's an easy path nearby."

"I've never done that before. Is it hard?"

"No. It's soothing…quiet and peaceful."

She'd been working all night and he wanted to take care of her. Between the moon and his flashlight, they'd be able to see. He gestured for her to stay put in the H2 while he got their gear together. "Would you like some hot cocoa?"

"Yes, please."

He grabbed the Thermos and poured a cup for each of them. She smiled up at him but quickly glanced away. She was nervous. It reassured him in ways it really shouldn't have.

He started to tip his cup toward hers in a silent toast, but she stopped him. "To living large and finding happiness."

He tapped the rims of their glasses together, his eyes never leaving hers. She had the most expressive eyes. He should warn her that her secrets were there for any man to see. To delve into and take advantage of.

He knew that living large with Lauren was dangerous. More so than any out-of-control ride down a racetrack.

He turned away, taking a deep swallow. How had she turned the tables? And how could he regain control? "I made soup for later."

"From a can?" she asked with that spark in her eye that said "men can't cook."

"Never."

"Takeout?"

"No."

"Well…"

"What?" he asked, sorting through the gear and getting the sticks ready for them to use.

She narrowed her eyes. "Come on, fess up. You can cook."

He shrugged at her. He didn't want to discuss it, but he liked to eat and had never really stayed put long enough to find decent take-out places.

"Where'd you learn to cook? Your mom?" she asked.

"No. In a night class," he said, handing a pair of snowshoes to her. He gave her some brief instructions on how to snowshoe.

"Why?" she asked in that quiet way of hers.

Never talk about old lovers with a potential one. Years of navigating the dating scene had made it easy to lie. At least in the past. With Lauren things were different. "Um…I wanted to."

"Oh, I see. Was she blond, brunette or redheaded?"

"Blond actually." He put his shoes on and led her away from the vehicle.

Lauren laughed. He stopped to look at her. She had one of those laughs that made him want to say screw it and leave off these trappings of seduction. He wanted her. Learning each other's secrets could come later.

"Pitiful, I know, but I really liked the cooking lessons, which have lasted longer in my life than she did."

"I hope so, since you invited me out. Unless you're planning on starting a harem."

"Too much trouble. Pleasing women takes a lot of energy."

"I'm not sure I like being lumped in a group like that. I'm very low-key. Very undemanding."

"How do you figure?"

She stopped and toyed with the charm on her necklace. In the moonlight she seemed untouchable. "I wouldn't have asked you to take a cooking class with me. I always delve into his interests."

Jack stopped, too. Lauren wasn't the kind of woman who doubted herself in any situation. He knew there was something important in what she was telling him but had no idea what. "Why?"

"I like learning new things. And… Never mind."

"Tell me, Lauren. You can trust me."

She shook her head, those thick tresses spilling over her shoulders, and then she looked up at him. Right in the eye. "I know I'll always have something lasting when the relationship ends."

She took a step away from him. Her tracks were the only ones in the thick layer of snow. "My mom says that it's because I don't believe a real man can live up to my dream man."

"What do you think?" he asked. He followed her easily.

"I think Mom puts too much stock in the books she's read. But I can't say that to her."

"Then why do you do it?"

"I'm not sure."

"I have a theory."

"You've only known me a few days. I'm not sure you have enough info to make an observation."

"Do you want to hear it or not?"

She glanced over her shoulder at him. A light snow began to fall. He took his scarf off and wrapped it around her neck. "Okay."

"I think it's because of your job."

"What?"

"I've been listening to your show, and you have this aura of intimacy with your listeners. And I think that's why you set yourself up for failure in relationships."

"You don't know—"

He put his finger over her lips to stop the words. She was defensive and he couldn't blame her. Soul baring wasn't really on the menu tonight.

"You don't have to defend yourself. It was only my opinion."

Lauren knew she'd said too much and strove to put some distance between them again. They talked of books and music. Jack set an easy pace through the park. She wasn't surprised to learn that he never kept any books or CDs for more than a few months. She couldn't imagine not having her favorite novels in her house so that she could reread them when the urge struck.

But that didn't stop her from remembering what he'd said—she did fear intimacy. She'd spent her entire life making sure there was some barrier between her and others. The radio was the ultimate cocoon, and she honestly didn't think she could work in another field.

The morning was beautiful and unexpected, but she was chilled by the time they returned to the Hummer H2. He turned on the heat and handed her a mug of vegetable soup. He shifted closer to her on the seat and she scooted away, then realized she was once again running away after she'd vowed to stop doing that.

"Tonight was your last night on the midnight shift?" he asked.

Lauren leaned back against the seat, letting the warmth from the heated leather surround her. "Yes. I'm moving to the morning drive time starting Monday."

"With your voice and your empathy you ought to do well there."

She knew he was right. Ty had been bugging her for years to move to the early slot, where she'd get more listeners. But Lauren liked the anonymity of doing the midnight show. She had some loyal fans but it was a small fan base. "I guess. Ty is moving me to help with the station's Valentine's Day promo."

"That Mile of Men thing. You know that's reverse sexism. If I sponsored a Mile of Women, you'd go nuts."

She had to laugh because she was coming to know Jack. He wasn't at all what she'd first expected him to be. Especially when it came to women. He wasn't a hound, as she'd expected. In fact, he had a deep well of caring that surprised her. "I know. You're right. But hey, that's acceptable in society now."

"Going to ride that wave while you can?" he asked. He stretched one arm along the back of the seat. She'd deliberately sat close to the door to keep some space between them.

"Men did it for a long time. It's our turn." Though she didn't really have a scorecard that she kept in the battle of the sexes. She suspected Jack didn't either.

"So will you be cruising that mile for men? Is that why Ty moved you?"

"Partly. I also challenged my listeners to help me find Mr. Right."

"What am I, chopped liver?"

She knew he meant it lightly but she couldn't treat it or him that way. She did want him.

"Not chopped liver. I can't decide what you are, Jack."

He dropped his arm around her shoulder and tugged her closer to him, pulling her into the shelter of his body. She knew that it made no sense, but the last of her chill faded when she was tucked up against him. This was her fantasy moment. She wanted to curl up against him. Let his warmth wrap around her body while his scent and his voice wrapped around her other senses.

"You look scared. I'm not going to pounce." He reached out and twirled a strand of her hair around his finger. Men always did that. Her curly ringlets seemed a temptation few could resist.

"I'm not afraid." Because the time for hedging had passed, and she knew without a doubt that she wasn't leaving tonight until they'd made a decision to go forward and pursue the attraction between them.

"Then what is it?" he asked. He tugged a few more strands into his hand so that her hair was wrapped around his fingers.

"Promise not to laugh?" she asked. Why did it matter? Her brother Duke always said she worried too much what others thought. But then, he was a six-foot-four linebacker and she wasn't.

"Yes," he said, his voice dropping an octave. "I'd never laugh at you, Lauren."

Jack made her feel good. She put her soup mug on the floorboard. She wrapped her arms around her waist and looked up at him. "I just have this image in my head of me and you."

"Naked?" he asked, waggling his eyebrows. "Because that doesn't make me want to laugh, sweetheart. That makes me want to howl *hot damn*."

She shook her head. It would be so easy to let herself get distracted. To keep this thing between them light and fun. But then in six months she'd be alone again. *Don't forget that.*

"No. Though I like that one, too. This one is… well…"

He sighed. His free arm snaked around her waist

and he lifted her onto his lap. And she was where she wanted to be. The hand in her hair pushed her head down onto his shoulder. And dammit, his shoulder felt as if it were made to cushion her head. She closed her eyes and breathed deeply.

"Tell me, Lauren. Trust me with your secrets. I'll keep them safe."

She wrapped her one arm around his waist and closed her eyes. "This is it. My image was this. You holding me close."

"Anything else?"

"Well…"

"What?"

"I love your voice. In my dream you were reading to me."

"What was I reading?"

"Shakespeare sonnets."

"Woman, do I look like a sonnet kind of guy?"

"It was a fantasy," she said, wriggling to get off his lap.

He held her still, tipping her chin up with his free hand and then kissing her deeply, thoroughly. Making this fantasy more real than she'd ever imagined it could be.

He lifted his head after a long moment, and Lauren saw something in his eyes that spoke to her heart.

"I was never a huge fan of Shakespeare, but I do know a few lines from Marlowe's 'Helen of Troy.'"

She leaned her head on his shoulder and listened

to his voice. It rumbled in his chest. This was just about perfect. The evening, the voice. She felt as if she'd found that secret thing she'd been searching for.

"Was this the face that launched a thousand ships/ And burnt the topless towers of Ilium?/ Sweet *Lauren,* make me immortal with a kiss."

She tunneled her fingers in his hair and brought his mouth to hers. This time she took charge, pushing her tongue deep into his mouth. Tasting again the cocoa and the desire of this very strong man who called to her soul.

Lauren shifted over him, straddling his lap, and all thoughts of that Marlowe play slipped away. Her mouth moved over his. Jack held her scalp in his palms, holding her still while he explored her.

She moaned, and he wanted more from her. More sounds, more noises. More everything.

She pulled back and stared up at him. Her lips were swollen and wet from his mouth. Her pupils were dilated and her skin was flushed. Her breathing was rapid, and his mirrored hers.

"So I'm Helen?" she asked, her contralto voice even deeper than normal.

"Hell, yeah," he said.

He rubbed the back of her neck and then slid his hands down her back until he cupped her rump. He flexed his fingers against her hips and she rocked forward against his hard-on.

"God, woman, don't do that."

"Why not? It feels so good."

She let her head drop back as she moved against him. Her breasts thrust forward, her eyes closed. She had an earthy sensuality that he'd sensed listening to her on her show. Seeing it firsthand set him on fire.

Watching Lauren made him hotter than he'd ever been before. Her nipples hardened under her shirt. Jack used his hands in the middle of her back to bring her closer to him. He raised her shirt and licked her nipples.

She grabbed his head and held him closer to her. "More."

He bit lightly at her distended flesh, and when she moaned again he started suckling on her. Her thighs clamped tighter around his hips.

Her womanly scent surrounded him and he stopped thinking. She felt better than any woman he'd ever held. He freed the buttons of her shirt and pushed it aside.

Her bra of white lace demicups made him groan. He pushed the cups out of his way and then stopped to study her. She was watching him. Her nipples were hard and pointed. Her stomach contracted with each breath she took and her hips rocked slowly against his.

He kept one hand at the small of her back. Held her still so that he could feast on her as he wanted. First with his eyes. Just looking at the textures of her velvety-soft skin and the colors, pink and cream. She was so soft.

He lifted his free hand and rubbed his knuckle over first one exposed nipple and then the other. Leaning forward, he let his breath brush over her.

She held his head tighter and lifted her breasts. "Please…"

"I'll please you, sweetheart."

A song started playing and Jack started away from Lauren. "Oh, damn. My mother."

"What?"

Lauren pushed herself off his lap and scrambled for her purse. "Hi, Mom."

Jack was still dazed. What the heck had happened?

"No. I'm fine. I stopped to eat on the way home."

She had one hand on her hip and her breasts were still bare. He caressed one breast and she batted his hand away. "Okay, Mom. Love you, too."

She closed her phone and looked at him. "Uh…"

"Changed your mind?"

"Yeah. I mean—I know this is bad timing."

"It's okay. I really only meant to have a nice evening with you. Not have you."

"Oh, Jack," she said in that way of hers that made him ache to make promises he knew he couldn't keep.

She turned away and fastened her shirt. Jack took several deep breaths but his erection was still strong. He needed Lauren. But he could wait.

"Want dessert?"

"Would you mind taking me home?"

"Not at all."

"Your mom calls you after work?" he said to distract himself. His mom called both him and Ty every evening. And if one of them wasn't home or reachable by cell phone, the other one had to go find him.

"Yes. I swear she thinks I'm still twelve."

"My mom does the same thing."

"Really?"

"Yeah. She worries about her boys."

"That's sweet. What's she like?"

She looked vulnerable, and he could tell by the flush on her skin that she was battling sexual arousal as well.

"She's larger than life but in a different way than my dad is. She has the image in her head…I think it's some crazy Donna-Reed-meets-the-Jetsons mom. She's always baking and knitting and making things."

"She sounds great."

"She is. She just lives in a kind of fantasy world."

"My mom is totally into reality."

"I can see that about your mom. Is she anything like her television persona?"

"Yes. She's everything like that. But with my brother and I it's more personal. Sorry I didn't mention you on the phone, but she'd never have stopped asking questions and probably would have wanted to talk to you."

"And that would be bad?"

"Oh, yes. She'd ask you a million questions and then give you a rundown of my flaws. So that you can approach this relationship with your eyes open."

"Really?" he asked, moving closer to her. "What are Lauren's flaws?"

"Other than dreaming about a fantasy man…"

"Other than that."

"I think cooking should take only thirty minutes. I love shoes and don't care if I don't have an outfit that matches them. I won't wear a thong, no matter how much a man begs."

He tipped his head back to study her. He wanted to see her in a thong but he could live without that one. "I think meals should be enjoyed and lingered over like a beautiful woman. I love trying new things. I wouldn't wear a thong either."

Lauren laughed and leaned toward him. He pulled her tight against his chest and held her in his arms, letting the sound of her laughter fill the dark recesses of his soul.

Six

Lauren already didn't like the new shift, but that was because she'd had to get out of bed at four o'clock in the morning to be at the station by four-thirty.

Lauren took a sip of her chai and settled into the DJ booth with her notes in front of her. At night she seldom discussed the day's news stories unless one of her listeners wanted to, but the morning was different. People were relying on WCPD to deliver information on their way to work.

Her producer, Rodney, was sharing the booth with Didi Sera, Ray's producer. Ray was funny, and already Ty had mentioned they'd had a surge in listeners even though he'd only been in town a week.

There was something about his drop-dead style of blunt advice and acerbic wit that drew listeners. Even her mom had been listening to the show on the Web and had said that Ray was interesting.

"Morning, Lauren. You ready to do this thing?" Ray said as he entered the booth. He set a large Starbucks cup on the counter and reached for his headphones.

"Yes, I am. I'm not sure that you need me."

He tilted his head to the side. "I definitely need you here. That one is always on my case. She's usually nicer when there's another woman around."

"I can hear you, Ray," Didi said from the producer's booth.

"*Madon'*, see what I mean?"

Lauren fought the urge to laugh. She wasn't getting in the middle of whatever was going on between Ray and Didi.

"How's the Mile of Men sign-up going?" Lauren asked. She hadn't heard from Jack over the weekend. And it looked as if her internal radar was up to par. Once again she was falling for a guy who was going to let her down.

"Very slow," he said.

"Um…I did something on my show that worked for a while," she said.

"What?"

"I had them call in and set me up. Maybe we can model our Mile of Men after that. Have some eligible bachelorettes sign up to pick from the men. What do you think?"

"Sounds great. We'll start with you."

"Yeah, that'll help. There are tons of great guys in Detroit just waiting to date me," Lauren said.

"I'm sure there are," Ray said in a voice that was so kind. He was a nice man despite the fact that he was so bossy.

Lauren realized she might have revealed some of her insecurities in that last statement. "I'm kind of seeing someone now."

"Can you get him to be part of the lineup?" Ray asked.

"Five minutes," Rodney said.

"I don't know." Why had she blurted that out? Jack hadn't called her, and she wasn't sure he would again. But she was weary of blind dates. She couldn't face another one. "Why?"

"Well, if you pick him and things work out, that'll be a great promotion for next year's event."

She heard the promo for the morning show and the intro for herself start playing. She mouthed the words *thank you* to Rodney. She didn't want to discuss Jack with this DJ or with anyone else. She doubted he'd stand out on the street even to help Ty out.

"Good morning, Detroit. Let's welcome my new partner on the air—Lauren B, aka Miss Lonely Hearts. She's looking for a good man, and we need you to volunteer as part of our Mile of Men."

"That's right, Ray, I am looking for a good man. And I'm willing to bet so are a lot of other women in Detroit. So let WCPD do the screening and join us on Valentine's Day."

Lauren let Ray continue telling the rules and directing listeners to the Web site. The computer screen in front of her flashed up. *Chopped Liver on line two.*

Ray finished talking and pushed a button to play music. "We'll be taking callers who want to volunteer next."

Lauren hit line two, careful to make sure it wasn't on the air.

"This is Lauren."

"Still looking for a man?" Jack asked in his deep voice.

"Well, that is why I'm here." She didn't have to explain herself.

"Sorry I couldn't call over the weekend. Some of my old college frat brothers were in town and wanted to do the Detroit club scene."

"You don't have to explain." She was hurt, and no matter what he said, he couldn't make this right. The club scene—he'd probably gone home with some blonde who didn't care if he was a frog in prince's clothing.

"Yes, I do. I don't like hearing you on the air talking about finding Mr. Right."

"I don't really like to hear about you clubbing."

"Give me a chance, Lauren."

"Why should I, Jack? We both have too much baggage to make anything work between us. We're too different."

"You didn't feel wrong in my arms. I screwed up. To be honest, I was afraid to call you."

"You're not afraid of anything."

"I'm afraid of what you make me feel, Lauren. And that's saying a lot. Give me one more chance. Don't pick some stranger…" He trailed off, and she heard the sincerity in his voice.

"This is a radio thing. Not a real-life thing. I'm not going to cruise down that line of men and pick someone else."

"Promise?"

"I've got to go."

"I know. I like hearing your voice first thing in the morning."

"I'm glad," she said.

He laughed and disconnected the phone. Lauren shook her head. He was getting to her. But he was trying, and that made her feel…she wasn't sure entirely.

"Your boyfriend?" Ray asked.

She shrugged. "Who do you have in the queue?"

"We've got three people who might work out. One is a middle manager of a chain restaurant, another is a construction worker and the third is a pastry chef."

"Pastry chef?" Lauren asked.

"Yeah, what do you think?"

"Women love a man who can cook," she said,

thinking of Jack and his homemade soup. She was missing something important about him and hoped she figured it out before they both got hurt.

"That's what I was hoping. This is harder than I thought it would be."

"Yeah, who thought being matchmaker could be so hard."

"You have no idea how tough it can be," Ray said.

The music stopped and they went back on live. They talked to the three men on-air and got two more volunteers.

Lauren enjoyed the morning but was glad when it was time to leave the booth. She'd had enough of discussing relationships and talking to men and women who'd been single too long and couldn't find a mate. The comments she and Ray heard rang a little too true for Lauren's peace of mind and reminded her that Jack was still an unknown quantity.

Jack was waiting when she exited the building at the end of the day. Leaning against the hood of a sleek black Porsche, he watched. She hesitated when she saw him, and he knew he'd have to make up for not calling. He smiled and pushed away from the car.

"What are you doing here?"

"Apologizing in person. And taking you to lunch."

"How did you know I hadn't eaten?"

"I called Ty."

"Why?"

He shrugged. "So I can buy you lunch."

"Not today. I—"

"Lauren."

She glanced over her shoulder. Ray King ambled over to them. He wore a topcoat and glanced around the parking lot before stopping.

"Sorry to interrupt," Ray said, but Jack suspected the older man wasn't really sorry.

"No problem. Ray, do you know Jack Montrose?"

"Yes, we met in Ty's office the day I started. Nice to see you again."

"Same here. We were on our way to lunch. How can we help you?" Jack asked. He took a step closer to Lauren and put his arm around her waist.

"We have a remote broadcast this afternoon at the Fox Theatre with some new entries in the Mile of Men. Lauren has to be there."

Jack snorted.

"Will you stop that?" Lauren said.

"What's the problem?" Ray asked.

Jack realized he'd put her in a bad position. "Nothing. I just think it's a tad bit sexist to have a Mile of Men."

"You still thinking about a Mile of Women?" Lauren asked in a silky tone that warned him he better beware.

"Of course not. I just…"

"*Compare,* you're digging yourself deeper," Ray said, but there was laughter in his voice. "Why don't you come along? We could use a differing viewpoint."

"Uh, Ray, Jack has his own business to run. He can't just drop everything to come to a remote broadcast."

He knew she wanted space from him. And Jack also had dated enough women to know that if he let Lauren go now, he wasn't going to get her back.

"I'll do it. What time should we be there?"

"Four. Ciao."

"Ciao," Jack said, putting his hand under Lauren's elbow and leading her to the car.

"When did I agree to lunch?"

He dropped her arm. "I'm not forcing you, sweetheart. If you want to go eat alone, then be my guest."

He was tired of being the bad guy. Sure he'd acted like an ass, but he'd apologized.

"Sorry, Jack. I'm...I'd be happy to have lunch with you."

"Where are we going?"

"A little place just out of town—Molly's."

Lauren said little as he drove through the crowded streets. Soon they were out of the downtown traffic and Jack let the Porsche roar with her innate power. He loved a fast car. If he were a different man, he'd take Lauren out of the city and into the countryside. Driving neck-or-nothing and showing her what it meant to really be alive.

"Jack?"

"Hmm?"

"You missed the turnoff."

He cursed under his breath. Checked for traffic and spun the car in a one-eighty. It was a move that required the driver know both himself and his car. Jack knew both well. He glanced over at Lauren and saw her hands were knotted together in her lap, but she gave him a faint smile.

He felt ridiculous. Like a teenager who was showing off his daddy's car to a girl he wanted to impress. But hell, he did want to impress Lauren and everything he did was to that end.

"Wow," she said quietly. He really hoped she hadn't sensed anything other than a guy who was a motorhead.

"Sorry. I get lost in the power of the car sometimes."

"No problem. I drive a really boring compact. I think my wheels would fall off if I tried something like that."

"It helps to know what you're doing," he said, then realized he was raising a subject he didn't want to touch. His dad had taught him show moves before he'd been able to drive legally. Sometimes Jack felt like being the wild rebel most people believed Diamond Dave's sons should be.

She was staring at him. Probably wondering if you're going to try to jump the Porsche over some ravine, he thought with disgust.

With a shrug he said, "My lawyer has a hell of a time keeping my license."

She smiled at that. "I can't picture you on mass transit."

"God forbid. And Carl, my chauffeur, says I'm a horrible back-seat driver."

"I'd think you'd be more overcautious."

Jack parked the car and turned it off before he twisted in his seat to face her. "Because of my dad?"

"Yes," she said. A slight flush covered her cheeks, and he knew that she regretted her comment.

Jack knew he should help her out, but a part of him—the boy who'd gotten into fights just to prove his dad was still a man after he'd lost the ability to walk—wanted to see how she was going to handle this.

She cleared her throat. "I mean, he can't walk now because of that car accident."

"Thanks for explaining it to me. Ty and I have been wondering for a while why Dad can't walk."

She bit her bottom lip and crossed her arms over her chest. "Sarcasm. That's really nice. You know I wasn't trying to offend you."

Jack turned away from her. What could he say? First he didn't call her for two days and now he was… "Sorry. Sometimes I'm an ass."

She gave him a sweet smile. "I'm the same way about my parents. People actually call my dad Mister Doctor Belchoir. He's a Ph.D. in Egyptian Studies. It makes him nuts."

"What do you say we stop discussing our families?" he asked. He needed to find his footing with her. She had to be like every other woman he'd ever met. As soon as he figured her out, she'd stop fascinating him.

"Sounds good," she said, but there was a lingering hurt in her eyes.

He got out of the car and saw Lauren hesitating, her hand on the door handle. He realized she did that each time he picked her up. He opened the door and put his hand at her elbow to lead her into the restaurant. "Why were you watching me like that?"

"Like what?" she asked. A light snow began to fall. She paused, tipped her head back and let the snowflakes land on her face.

When she looked at him again, crystal drops beaded her face like diamonds sparkling in the sunlight. He forgot what he'd been saying. Leaning closer to her, he breathed in her scent and then licked the snowflakes from her face.

He held her face caged between his hands and he felt that if he could keep touching her, he wouldn't screw this up. If they could get into bed, he could stop trying to remember how he was supposed to act and just make love to this woman who wouldn't get out of his head.

"You were saying something about the car," she said after a long minute had passed.

He was? He dropped his hands to his side and recalled what he'd been thinking before. "Like you weren't sure I was going to get your door. You know I will."

"In the beginning most guys do. Then they stop. I wasn't sure…."

He held the door to the building open for her. "I'm not most guys, Lauren. Which that stunt with the car should have proven. What am I going to have to do? Jump over four parked cars? Juggle fire?"

"Can you juggle fire?" she asked, taking off her coat and hanging it on one of the hooks by the door.

"Yeah," he said. He shed his coat and hung it up, as well.

"Don't," she said, pulling him to a stop.

"Don't what?"

"Don't pretend that I'm different. I'll start believing you."

"Good."

"Not good, Jack. Painful. Why didn't you call me for two days? I waited by the phone believing… well, believing something that I know better than to believe in."

Lauren followed Jack into the restaurant. She'd play it cool during lunch. She'd had guys not call before, so it wasn't that. It was that he kept talking about being her knight in shining armor and she'd started to believe him.

The hostess took their drink order and Lauren studied the menu, not really seeing the words.

The menu was taken from her hands. Jack placed it on top of his and took her hands in his. "I'm sorry."

Let it go, she thought. But another part of her wanted to push as hard as she could and make him feel as bad as she had. "For?"

"Not calling."

"No biggie. I told you it wasn't the silence that bothered me, it was…" She wasn't going to say it again.

"Remember what you said about your mom, when we went snowshoeing?"

She nodded. She couldn't talk right now because there was a pain and anger in his voice that she inherently understood. It spoke to her where she was waiting to get hurt again by a man she'd already started caring for.

"Well, my mom is the same way. I had to threaten Ty to keep you a secret from her."

"Are you not sure about me?" she asked.

"No, I'm sure about you. So sure I don't want my wacky family scaring you away."

She understood what he wasn't saying. That family expected things when you introduced them to someone new, and sometimes you weren't ready for those expectations. "That doesn't forgive me for not calling."

"Really, it's okay. I'm sorry I brought it up."

"Are you ready to order?"

Lauren glanced at the waitress who stood impatiently by their table.

"No. We'll need a few minutes," Jack said.

The waitress left. Jack didn't let go of her hands.

He didn't say anything, just held them and watched her face. And for the first time she felt as if she was enough for a man. That there was no test she had to pass. No skill she needed to acquire. Nothing more was required of her than just being herself.

She tugged her hands free and picked up her menu. "Have you eaten here before?"

"Yes. The food is first-rate. You can't go wrong with any of the daily specials."

"Unless you're on a low-carb diet," she said automatically. She'd always been a little chunky and sometimes still felt as if she should be on a diet. Not all the time, but when she sat across from Jack, who looked as though he'd just posed for the cover of *Men's Health* with his rock-hard abs displayed… well, she wasn't feeling up to par bodywise.

"Are you?" he asked. She felt his gaze move over her body.

"No. I can't give up carbs. I try to get out and run…well, I was going to lie and say every day, but I hope you'll see me naked someday and that means you'll know I don't run every day."

He laughed and she was glad she'd lightened the mood. "I like a woman who's soft."

"Is that a euphemism?" she asked.

He waited until she met his gaze before he answered and she saw the sincerity in his eyes. "Nope. It's the truth. There's something very feminine about curves instead of steel-hard muscles."

She took his words to heart. She wasn't ever going to have big muscles. She didn't like to work out and she really didn't like to exercise. But running was fun, and she usually could coax her neighbor two houses down, a writer, to go with her. Jane kept the same odd hours Lauren did, so jogging in the middle of the afternoon suited her.

"Tell me about the gig I agreed to for this afternoon."

"What do you want to know?" she asked.

"Just the basics."

"We'll put the hunky guys on the air and let them talk a bit about themselves and what they want in a woman. Ray likes to stir things up, so I'm betting he's going to put you on, too."

"Hunky guys?"

She arched her eyebrows at him. "Oh, yeah."

Their food arrived and they talked about their likes and dislikes in music. She found out that he had extremely eclectic tastes but really loved old Motown, which was why he'd started his own record label.

"I like Barry Manilow. It's my deep, dark secret but there it is. My friend Beverly and I try to get to at least one concert of his each tour," Lauren admitted.

"A Manilow groupie. You've shocked me."

"Don't say it like that. He writes the songs the whole world sings."

"Please don't start."

"Start what? I bet you like at least one of his songs."

"Men don't like Barry Manilow."

She giggled at that. He was so serious, but she saw a glint of humor in his eyes. "That's silly. I bet if I started singing the beginning to 'Copacabana,' you'd join in."

"That's a bet you'd lose. But you're welcome to try it."

She shook her head. "Sorry, but you're going to have to earn the privilege of hearing my Copa rendition."

"I'll make that my new goal," he said.

It was a silly promise to have made but it fit this moment and this man. He made it so easy to just be herself that she forgot all about those dating books her mom had sent her over the years and the advice in them. She forgot that every man she'd ever really liked had left. She forgot that Jack thought he was a prince in toad's clothing.

Seven

The Fox Theatre had been part of an urban-renewal project and now shone like an empress on Woodward Avenue. Jack glanced around for Lauren, not sure she'd arrived yet. He'd dropped her off at the station earlier to get her car.

He checked his watch for the third time and then forced himself to stop.

"Sorry I'm late," Lauren said from behind him.

He glanced over at her. She made him feel good inside, and he knew better than to indulge in those feelings.

"Ty's coming, too."

"Great. That's just what I need, my little brother

hanging around while I'm romancing you," he said.

"Is that why you're here—so you can romance me?"

"I know better than to answer that question."

"But you don't know better than to say that?" she asked, but he knew she was playing with him. There was no anger in her voice. She liked to needle him as much as he liked having her do it.

"What's wrong with romance?"

"Nothing. Except that men seem to think it's a chore and something they have to do."

"Ah, sweetheart, there's nothing about you that's a chore."

"Really?" she asked. Her eyes went wide and she tilted her head to the side, something he noticed she did when she was trying to figure him out.

Damn, was he showing her his own vulnerabilities? He didn't want her to realize that romance was really all he was good for. He was an expert at saying and doing the right things—for a while. He'd never been able to figure out when romance was no longer enough in a relationship.

He leaned over to kiss her, because she tempted him to believe in some things that he knew weren't real.

She sighed into his mouth, tasting faintly of the exotically spiced tea he knew she drank. Her hands against his neck were cold but her mouth under his was hot.

He tipped her head farther back, opening her completely for his invasion. It was a calculated move to show her his supremacy. She tightened her fingers on his shoulders, her nails scoring him through the thin layer of his oxford shirt.

He snaked one arm around her waist and lifted her into his body. She didn't struggle but undulated against him, making him realize that his control was an illusion. He hardened in a rush as she rubbed her hips lightly over his.

"Get a room," Ty said.

Jack didn't lift his mouth from Lauren's but reached around her and socked his brother in the shoulder. Lauren pulled away. Her lips were swollen and wet from his kisses.

God, he needed more than a few moments with her. He needed her naked under him. More and more he was beginning to believe that was the only way he'd be able to figure her out.

"What are you doing here?" Ty asked. "I thought you weren't the type to publicly humiliate yourself over a woman."

Jack groaned. Ty was clearly in a very good mood, which meant his brother was going to be very annoying. "Lauren, sweetheart, would you look away for a minute?"

"Why?"

"So I can twist my brother's arm and make him behave."

"Beating up your little brother…I thought you'd

outgrown that," Ty said. "He always was a big bully."

Lauren just laughed and put herself firmly between the two of them.

"Actually I'm here because your PR gal, Misty Rogers, said she'd pick me off the line of men."

Lauren took Jack's hand, leading him over to Ray and his producer, Didi. Jack watched her work, wishing they could get out of the theatre. Go someplace quiet.

He stopped thinking of romance and seduction and just forgot about all the things he knew to do with women. He went to her and put his arms around her, pulled her back against his chest. She reached into her purse and pulled out a CD. Over her shoulder he saw that she was holding *Manilow Scores*.

"Your secret obsession will be known to the world if you carry that around."

"It's a gift for you," she said, slipping the CD into his overcoat pocket. "I think my secret obsession has changed."

Jack brought dessert and opened a bottle of wine while she put the finishing touches on dinner later that night. Lauren enjoyed working with him in the kitchen. So much of what she thought of as home seemed to center around food. Every dish she prepared reminded her of someone in her family.

"I like this. After your 'quick cooking' comment, I wasn't expecting such a well-equipped kitchen."

Lauren glanced around. She'd inherited a lot of her grandmother's kitchen machines and gadgets.

"You shouldn't rush to judgment."

"I'm learning that with you," he said. "Who's in that picture over the phone?"

She glanced at the photo of the small storefront grocer with her great-grandmother standing in front of it. The black-and-white photo had been taken in 1918 at the store her grandparents ran in Brooklyn. "My great-grandmother."

Jack went over to study the picture, looking completely at home. Only when they sat down at the table to eat did Lauren feel awkward. The day had been a strange one and she was still adjusting. She was also tired from the early-morning shift.

"This is good. I had no idea such results were possible in only thirty minutes," he said.

"Flattery will get you everywhere," she said.

"It's sincere."

"I know." And she did know. Or was starting to get to know him well enough to recognize that Jack didn't tell social white lies.

She noticed he hadn't stopped looking at her kitchen walls, which were covered in pictures. She had some prints that Duke had sent her from Florence. Some pictures of her parents grilling at their house. Some of her brother and his family. She settled deeper into her seat and realized that she'd surrounded herself with them.

What was his family like? She didn't want to ask him any questions, given the way he'd reacted when she'd mentioned his father's accident earlier today. But then, she knew he didn't like to share anything personal. Those details seemed to slip out unexpectedly.

"My grandmother taught me to cook. My mom was always too busy to learn, and Grandma thought she'd never have a girl to teach what she'd spent a lifetime perfecting. I can't explain it, but it was so special when I was with her in the kitchen."

"Your family is full of traditions and togetherness," he said. In his voice she heard something that sounded almost like longing, but that couldn't be right. Jack Montrose had everything any red-blooded American man could want. Why would he envy her?

She'd never thought about it but he was right. Her family had a ton of traditions that were more like rituals sometimes. "I'm sure you do, too. Didn't you say your mom called all the time?"

"Yes, but my family is nothing like yours. My mom was an orphan and my dad...well, let's just say he had a falling out with his family before he made it big."

Lauren's heart ached at what he didn't say. Only because she knew Ty as well did she realize how little family the Montrose men had. It was really the two of them and their mom. "Did they accept him once he was famous?"

"They tried to. But old Dave wasn't one to forgive and forget, so he said screw them—except with more vulgarity—and we haven't spoken to them since."

"I could talk to my mom if you all want to go on her show. She's big into healing those kinds of rifts."

"No. We're not really into the spotlight."

"Why not?"

"Probably because my dad always went after it," Jack said. She knew he didn't want to say more. She remembered a picture in Ty's office of him and Jack wearing identical American-flag suits and standing next to motorbikes. Though she wasn't going to ask any more questions, she'd bet that they had been made to perform after their father's accident. How people could treat their own kin so shabbily she couldn't understand.

"I'm sorry you didn't have any grandparents. My grandfather loved to spoil Duke and me. He was always slipping us candy and cutting up with us at the dinner table. I can't imagine not having that."

"You don't miss what you never had."

Jack didn't say anything else but continued eating his meal.

"Thanks for the Manilow CD."

"Did you listen to it?"

"Hell, no. I told you men don't like him."

"Ha. How about I send you a CD you will like?"

"Of what?"

"My biggest requests."

"You have that?"

"Yes. Last Christmas the station made a CD of my show and we sold them for ten dollars for charity. All of your favorites are on there."

"How do you know that?"

"Because they're all slow and sexy. Marvin Gaye, Stevie Ray Vaughan…all the ones you commented on when you picked me up that first night."

"Must be why I like you," he said, putting down his fork.

"Why?"

"Because you are sweet and sexy."

She couldn't respond to that because she knew where this evening was leading and a part of her was afraid to let him any closer to her than he already was.

Lauren's phone rang just as they finished dinner. She glanced at the caller ID. "It's my mom. Do you mind?"

"Not at all. I'll give you some privacy," he said, crossing her living room and opening the glass door.

He stood on her small patio and listened to the sounds of the evening. The snow that had fallen earlier coated her backyard. It was chilly but he enjoyed that. It helped him focus on something other than Lauren.

But that only worked for a few minutes. He liked her house. It was cozy and reflected the woman who lived there. Her family was obviously a close one. The pictures didn't stop in the kitchen but covered the walls of her hallway and the mantel over her fireplace.

Though she'd said she was searching for Prince Charming, he knew she wasn't searching for love. She already had that in spades. He wished his parents could see her house. Then maybe they'd understand that what they were searching for couldn't be found in the places they'd been looking.

That finding a new mate and trying again wasn't the answer to the family life they both had always been seeking. He rubbed the back of his neck.

"Want some hot chocolate?" Lauren asked from the doorway.

He pivoted to face her. She was silhouetted by the light that spilled from the living room, her thick hair curling around her face and falling on her shoulders. She canted one hip to the side and stood there in her stocking feet, looking more desirable than any fashion runway model.

"It's kind of a yes-or-no question," she said, holding her hand out to him.

He wanted to take it. But at the same time, he didn't want to go back into her homey little house and exchange more small talk. Or reveal any more details of his own dysfunctional clan. He wanted to get past this getting-to-know-you stage and get to the hello-naked stage.

"Yes, I want something hot," he said, taking her hand, tugging her closer to him. He saw her shiver and knew he should just go inside.

But he liked the idea of providing warmth for

her, keeping her toasty on a cold night, so instead he drew her into his arms. Rubbing his hands up and down her back, he held her until she stopped shivering. He liked the way her curves felt against his body.

"Will you mind if it's powdered stuff? Actually it's kind of embarrassing, but I love the kind with the little marshmallows in it."

"You're rambling," he said. She must be nervous. He understood why. The mood had changed between them, and he suspected they both knew where they wanted the evening to end. But getting there always took some steps that could be slow and laborious.

"What were you thinking about out here?" she asked, tipping her head up toward his.

He leaned down. She had the most kissable mouth he'd ever seen. He brushed his lips lightly back and forth over hers. Her hands slid up around his shoulders, holding him.

She traced the seam of his lips with her tongue, and her fingers caressed the ridge of his ear. He wanted her with a bone-deep certainty that made nothing else matter.

She rose on her tiptoes, opened her mouth over his and kissed him. For the first time he allowed her to control the embrace. And he liked it. She wasn't shy or tentative, but she also didn't shove her tongue down the back of his throat. She tasted him with long, languid sweeps of her tongue. He moved his hands up and down her back and let the slow movements of her mouth dictate the mood and the moment.

It felt good to let things slow down. To enjoy just the taste and feel of each other. His blood flowed heavier in his veins and he no longer felt the chill of the air. He was getting hotter, heavier, and there was only one cure for what ailed him.

He held it in his arms. She pulled back and looked up at him with her wide eyes, and he knew that he didn't want to go home tonight.

She brought her hands up to cup his face. Ran her fingers over the slight stubble on his cheeks. He turned his face in her hands. God, she had the softest touch.

He wanted to stand here with her like this forever.

"What were you thinking about?" she asked again.

"How much I want you," he answered honestly. "In fact, I want you a hell of a lot more than I want hot chocolate."

She bit her lower lip. "Want to watch a movie?"

He shook his head.

"Want to watch me?" she asked.

"What will you be doing?"

"Seducing you with secrets learned from a harem girlfriend of mine."

"First rambling, now silly. If you're nervous or unsure, I'll leave."

"Do you want to leave?" she asked, her voice dropping, becoming that husky alto that stroked him like a velvet glove.

"No, sweetheart. I want to stay here all night."

She took a step back and led him into the house. Down the short hallway into her bedroom. "I wasn't being silly about the harem friend. I'm going to knock your socks off, Jack."

"Hot damn."

Eight

Lauren turned on the lamp on the nightstand before facing Jack. He stood where she'd left him just inside her bedroom. He toed off his shoes and stooped to remove his socks.

She liked that he wasn't shy about…well, anything. Despite his manners and sophistication, at heart Jack was a pretty basic man.

"Okay, my socks are knocked off. Let's get to it."

"Give me a break."

"What?"

"Does that line ever work?"

"I'm testing new material with you."

"Why?"

"Because the old stuff doesn't feel right with you."

She was flattered. "Sit on the bed."

He did as she asked. There were about ten pillows at the head of the bed. Jack carefully arranged them behind his back and then crossed his hands behind his head and leaned back.

"I'm ready," he said. It was arrogant—a command from a man who knows he's in charge.

"I'm not," she said. She still wore the jeans and sweater she'd put on this morning for work. Not exactly seductive clothing. But then, Lauren had found that a feeling of sexiness came from inside.

She lit the candles that were on her dresser and on her nightstand and then turned off the light. The room filled with a soft ambient light. Then she entered her closet and took off her clothes.

Her chest of drawers was in the back, and she pulled out a sheer thigh-length negligee. She slipped that on and reentered the bedroom.

Jack let out a wolf whistle and waggled his eyebrows at her. "Very nice."

He made her feel sexy. She knew she didn't look like a model, but she was a woman and she knew how to have a good time in bed.

The scents of her candles filled the room. Jack had removed his shirt and belt while she'd been changing. She skimmed her gaze over the planes of his chest. There was a light dusting of hair that tapered as it moved over his flat stomach.

His pants were unbuttoned but still zipped. He looked like a decadent pasha waiting to be served. His chest rose and fell with each breath he took. His nipples were hard and his skin flushed. His erection strained against his pants and she knew he was anything but relaxed.

She went to the CD player to draw out the anticipation. Flipping through the stack of albums that spanned every genre and generation of music, she settled on Norah Jones's soft, sultry love songs.

"If that's Manilow, I'm taking charge."

She shook her head, enjoying the feel of her long hair against the back of her neck. Then glanced over her shoulder at him. He was staring at her butt.

She dropped the CD case and bent over to pick it up. He bolted off the bed in a split second. "Enough teasing me. The mood is set. The only thing left is for you to get your sweet butt on the bed."

Before she could respond, he picked her up. Two steps later he dropped her on the bed and put his hand on her stomach to hold her in place, lowering himself between her legs.

"That's much better than candles and music," he said.

He held her wrists in one of his hands up above her head. He lowered his face to her neck, kissing and lightly biting her skin as he moved down her torso.

She tried to free her hands but he tightened his grip. Instead she slid one of her legs between his, caressing the back of his thigh and calf with her toes. She loved the rough feel of the hair on his legs and the tough sinew underneath.

She arched up into him. He groaned deep in his throat, a sound that was almost animalistic.

He traced random patterns on the globe of her breast with his tongue, coming closer and closer to her aching nipple but always turning away before his tongue touched her.

"Jack. Please." She shifted her shoulders, trying to move her nipple closer to his lips.

"Please what, sweetheart?" He lifted his head, resting his chin on her sternum and staring up at her.

"Please stop torturing me," she said.

"I thought that was what all this was for." He shifted his head, indicating the candles and pillows. His hair rubbed sensuously over her skin. Every part of her body felt full, heavy, enervated. She needed more of him touching her everywhere.

"You thought wrong."

He leaned to the left, and she felt his warm breath across the tip of her breast. Her nipple tightened even more, aching now. She arched her back and tried to twist toward him, but he lifted himself up on his elbow.

"Dammit."

"Tsk-tsk. I'm in charge now."

"You were always in charge," she said.

"How?"

"Never mind," she said. She felt like a fool. She

was almost naked and totally vulnerable to this man. She didn't want to give him any other tools to use against her.

He lowered his head and kissed her. One of those long, drugging kisses of his that made her forget to breathe. And it didn't matter because he was breathing for her. She wrapped her legs around his hips and wished she could do the same with her arms.

She held him close to her. But still wanted him closer, needed him to get rid of the layers of cloth between the two of them and thrust into her body. Only then would she be happy. Feel complete.

He lifted his head, his erection rock-hard against her. Her center was wet, ready for him. But he didn't make a move toward speeding up their lovemaking.

"Why did you do all this?"

She closed her eyes. He wasn't going to let it go.

"Because you've had a hundred lovers and I don't want to get lost in the sea."

He cursed softly but with a savage intensity that almost frightened her. He freed her wrists and captured her face in his hands. "You could never be part of a sea. You are the only woman who's ever called to me."

Her words made him want to lay claim to her, body and soul. The playful air that she'd tried to create dropped away. He understood a little too late what she'd been doing, and that made him want to cradle her in his arms and swear he'd protect her.

Swear an oath like one of the knights in those fairy tales she dreamed about. But he knew that celibacy would play no part in any of his vows and that tonight he had to show her in no uncertain terms exactly what she meant to him.

He knew the price he'd pay. Leaving himself vulnerable to her…well, it wasn't something he wanted to contemplate.

Her hands rested on his chest, toying with the strands of hair there. Tiny shivers danced down his spine. He closed his eyes, grappling for control. "Have I made you wish you'd gone home?"

He rubbed his erection against the center of her body. "Does this feel like it?"

"Well, what are you waiting for?"

He pushed the thin material covering her body up and over her head, tossing it away with a flick of his wrist. He leaned back then and just stared at her. She was beautiful to him already, her physical form the last piece in completing the masterpiece that was Lauren.

Her skin had a natural olive tone to it and her breasts were full but not large, topped with those tempting pink nipples that he'd been dying to taste. Her legs were long and smooth. He skimmed one hand down her left leg. Her toes were painted a fiery red and there was a toe ring on her second toe.

He lifted her foot, caressing the slim gold band. "Who gave you this?"

"I did. I just turned thirty, and it seemed appropriate."

He wanted to cover her in jewels. To mark her on the outside as his so that every man who saw her knew she wasn't available.

But it was too soon for that. And he wasn't the possessive type. He nibbled his way up her leg, stopping when he reached the top of her thigh. He could smell her arousal and it made him see red. He was ready for her.

He pushed her thighs farther apart and lowered his head to taste her. He parted her with his thumbs. She moaned and her hands clutched at his head, her hips lifting toward his mouth.

Groaning, he leaned forward and tasted her. She was hot and spicy. He took her hands from his head and pushed them up her body, over her breasts. He massaged her with her own hands as he continued to feast on her very delicate flesh.

She thrashed on the bed under him. She caressed her breasts without his encouragement and he skimmed his hands down her body. Grabbing her butt, he lifted her up higher, opened her wider to his questing tongue. Tasted her deeper. Her body started to tighten around his tongue and then she shuddered.

He slid up her body, tasting every inch of her skin. She scratched her nails down his back and around his waist to his zipper. She pushed his pants down his hips, then pushed them off with her feet.

She repeated the move with his boxers. He almost came when she lifted herself up against him. The movement made her entire body undulate against his, and it was the last straw.

He positioned himself and entered slowly. She was hot and wet and so damned tight. He froze as he realized he'd totally forgotten a condom. He pulled out of her body. He hadn't brought any condoms with him tonight. And that wasn't like him.

Dammit.

"What's the matter?" she asked. Her eyes were slumberous. Her body flushed with desire and her hips lifted, rubbing her wetness over his erection.

He groaned, thrusting against her.

"Protection?" he asked. *Grunted* would be a more accurate description. He could barely think, much less speak.

"I'm on the Pill," she said, reaching between them and taking him in her hand. She caressed the length of him and then rubbed her finger over the tip.

She drew him to her opening, and he tightened his grip on her hips and thrust inside. It was like coming home. He stopped thinking. He knew the sounds she made in her climb to orgasm now and held on until he heard them.

Her legs tightened around his waist and she made that small gasp as she climaxed. He lifted her hips higher so he could go deeper, thrust all the way home.

Then his orgasm washed over him and he called

her name. He rested on her as they both came back to earth, her breasts a soft pillow under his head. He turned and flicked her nipple with his tongue.

There was still so much he wanted to do with her. He shifted them to their sides and suckled her pretty breasts while her hands swept up and down his back.

Then she hugged him tight to her. He lifted his head and saw that her eyes were closed. She bit her bottom lip and held him with a fierceness that made his own heart ache.

It was too soon to feel this much for her. But at the same time he knew it was too late. He felt her vulnerability to him. Felt her need for him. He needed her the same way, needed to protect her from any hurts—even the ones he might deliver.

But not tonight. Tonight he wanted to keep the focus light. Pretend that nothing had changed, even though he knew in his gut that everything had.

"You definitely knocked my socks off," he said.

"Ditto," she said, lowering her mouth to his.

He knew she didn't want to talk and that suited him, as well. So instead he made love to her again, all the while hoping that this would be enough.

Lauren woke up alone when the alarm went off at three-thirty. God, she really hated this new shift. She stretched, feeling small aches from the night before. She rolled over, burying her face in the pillow that Jack had slept on. It still held his scent.

She hugged it to her breast and kept her eyes shut. There was no going back and pretending now. She was falling in love with Jack.

Where was he? She couldn't believe he'd be out of bed already. Maybe if she kept her eyes closed, she could stay in the pleasant dreamworld where reality couldn't intrude.

The light in the hallway came on and a minute later he entered her room. "Morning."

She lowered the pillow and opened her eyes. Jack was sitting on the side of the bed wearing only his pants and holding two coffee cups. He had a great chest.

"Morning," she said. She hoped her hair wasn't sticking up.

He handed her one of the cups and she realized it was the chai tea she liked to drink. She knew he was a coffee drinker. "Sorry I don't have coffee."

"That's okay, I didn't come here for the coffee," he said. He propped some pillows against the headboard and leaned back.

"What did you come here for?" she asked. So much for keeping things light. But she needed to know. She wanted to cushion what she was feeling by tempering it with what she could expect from Jack. And though he'd warned her not to paint him with the same brush that she had other men she'd dated, it was hard not to.

He was more intense than those other guys. He made her feel alive and wish for things that she'd been slowly trying to stop wishing for.

"For you, Lauren. Just for you."

She took another sip of her tea. She almost believed him. Had he woken up early or never gone to sleep? She suspected he hadn't slept. "You didn't have to get up early."

"I wanted to."

She wasn't sure what to do. She wished she'd picked a better night to sleep with him for the first time. A night when she didn't have to rush out of the house to get to work. Because something wasn't right with Jack this morning, and she knew if she had a little more time, she could figure it out.

She got to her feet. "Want to join me in the shower?"

"How much time do you have?"

"Fifteen minutes, and I have to leave at four or I'll be late."

"I'd better skip."

She set her mug down on the dresser and gathered her underwear. "Will you be here when I get out?"

"Yes. I'm not leaving until you do."

"Okay." She hurried into the bathroom. Trying not to think about Jack or last night or the new feelings buzzing through her system, she focused on her routine.

When she came out of the bathroom ten minutes later, he was still reclining on her bed. He'd donned his shirt and turned on the lamp. He was reading one of the books she'd left on her nightstand.

Since her hair was naturally curly, she never blew it dry, so it was still damp. Her room was a little chilly but she ignored the cold and Jack, went into her closet and found a pair of jeans and a thick sweater.

She dressed and reentered the bedroom, glimpsing the cover of the book he was reading. It was one of the erotic novels she'd left there.

"Have you read this book?" he asked.

"Yes."

"Have you ever done anything like this?"

The storyline of the book was a dominant/submissive one where the woman was totally mastered by her lover. She was at his mercy, living only for his pleasure. And though Lauren liked to read those kinds of books sometimes, she didn't think she could be like that in real life.

"No."

"Too bad. I'd love to have you live for my pleasure."

"Would you be responsible for mine?"

"Of course."

"Somehow I'm not surprised by that. You're very old-fashioned when it comes to women."

"Hell, it's not other women who bring out those tendencies in me. It's you. And I'm damned possessive, too."

"You are?" she asked.

He nodded and pushed to his feet, tossing the book on the bed. "I was jealous of the thought of any other man treating you that way."

She shivered at the intensity in his eyes. "That's just pretend."

"Logically I know it, but you have to see how that would appeal to any man. To own a woman, body and soul. To have you take food from my hand, pleasure from my hand, serve only me. It's a heady thought, Lauren."

A part of her wanted that but she knew that it was a fantasy as much as finding that fairy-tale prince. It was a sexual fantasy where she didn't have to worry about body shape or image. Didn't have to worry about pleasing him, because in those books pleasure was always guaranteed.

"Don't worry, I'm not going to attempt to turn you into my sexual slave," he said, slipping his shoes on. "Are you free for lunch today?"

"I think so."

"Good. I'll drive you to work and pick you up at one?"

She nodded. They walked through the house and Lauren was very aware that he'd changed the subject. He held her jacket out for her and she put it on. His hands rested on her shoulders for a minute.

She turned in his embrace, lifting her hands up to cage his face. "If it was just for fun...only in the bedroom...I wouldn't mind being your sex slave."

Nine

"**G**ood morning, Detroit! You're listening to WCPD, the station that keeps the hits coming even when you're freezing your stuff off. This is Ray King and the lovely Lauren B., saying move your tush out of bed and get on your feet."

Lauren took another sip of her tea and listened to Ray riff. He really liked to talk and she enjoyed the energy he brought to the show. She glanced over to the producer's booth and saw Didi shaking her head. Lauren had the feeling that Didi had a hard time keeping Ray in line.

Rodney sent her a message on the computer screen telling her to break in and send them to commercial. Didi had left the booth. "Now that you're out of bed, you'll want to stay tuned for today's top news and more information on our Mile of Men. Ladies, today we're taking your calls on what makes a man Mr. Right versus Mr. Wrong."

She hit the commercial button and took off her headphones. Ray did the same.

"Did you see her face?"

"Yes. I think she's going to chew you out."

"Yeah, that one likes to think she can keep me in line," he said. The door opened behind him. "But it's like I'm always telling her—babe, you gotta give a man room to move."

"How many times am I going to have to ask you not to call me babe?" Didi asked.

"You gotta warn me when she sneaks up on me like that," Ray said to Lauren.

"Can you cover the calls while we have a chat outside?" Didi asked.

"Sure."

They left and Lauren heard them arguing back and forth before the door closed. She glanced at Rodney. He shrugged.

She put her headphones back on and cued her mike to the producer's booth. "It's just us for a while. Can you set it up so I get one right, one wrong? I don't want this to turn into a male-bashing session."

"Me either," Rodney said. "Why don't you start it

off? We've got three calls in the queue. You're back in five."

She nodded, listened to the commercial ending and then hit the button to put her on-air. "Finding that perfect mate can be hard in the twenty-first century, and no one knows that better than I do.

"My late-night listeners have been helping find that elusive animal, Mr. Right, and over the last few weeks they've given me all sorts of insight. And the one thing I've found to be true is that Mr. Perfect for one woman won't be the right guy for another one. So let's take your calls and see what makes up your personal wish list."

Ray eased back into the booth and put on his head-phones just as the first caller started to talk. She glanced at him and he gave her the thumbs-up.

The caller, Janice, was looking for a man who would be a partner to her and help raise her three kids. She'd been married twice before. "I'm not sure why I keep dating. I seem to always be attracted to the wrong guys."

"I hear you, Janice. I think we keep dating because we know that there is such a thing as a good match. Some sort of nice ever after more than happily ever after," Lauren said.

"Maybe you're going for flash instead of sub-stance," Ray said.

"What?"

"Do you date men because of how they act or how they look?" Ray asked.

"Well, it starts out with looks…."

"Start out with something else," Ray said.

"How can I?" Janice asked.

"The next time you see a guy you like, change things up. Instead of jumping right into the relationship, take it slow," Ray said.

"Becoming friends first helps in the long run," Lauren added.

"That makes sense. I'm going to give it a try."

"Great. Let us know how it works out," Lauren said. Ray smiled over at her and talked them into another commercial break.

Lauren felt a connection to her mother for the first time. She'd never really understood her mom's need to get people on television to talk out their problems. This morning, though, she was starting to see the benefits to that and it made her feel really good.

They took calls for the remainder of the morning. Ty was waiting in the hallway when they left the booth. "Good show. We've been getting calls all morning. Lauren and Ray, you guys are a hit."

"I guess asking to be switched back to midnight is going to be—"

"A no. Sorry Lauren. I need you here."

"Hey, babe, is it me?" Ray asked.

"No, it's the hour. I'm not really a morning person."

"Hell, who is?" Ray asked.

"I am," Didi said from behind him, making Ray jump.

"*Madon'*, babe, you gave me a heart attack."

"I'm going to give you more than that if you don't stop calling me babe."

Ty laughed and stepped between them. "The promotions department needs to see you all upstairs for a new photo for the billboards. Lauren, you have a guest in your office. You've got fifteen minutes."

Rodney, Didi and Ray left, but Ty stayed behind. "Who's my guest?"

"Jack."

"Oh."

"I want to warn you about my brother."

Lauren closed her eyes. "Please don't. I know he's not the long-haul kind of guy."

Ty sighed and patted her arm. Lauren assumed he meant the gesture to be comforting. "Don't worry about me."

"I'm worried about both of you. Be careful," Ty said as they got on the elevator.

The doors opened on the floor where her office was. She got off, aware that Ty stayed on. Jack was seated in her guest chair, skimming through a copy of her mother's latest book.

She hesitated in the doorway, knowing that despite Ty's warnings and her own instincts, it was too late. She was already too involved with a man who might not be Mr. Right. But dammit, he sure as hell seemed as though he was.

* * *

Jack heard Lauren behind him and didn't turn around. He'd listened to her show this morning, very aware that he could be one of the men those women had called in about. For Mr. Wrong. Part of the problem was that women today analyzed things too much.

It pissed him off because he wanted to really sit back and enjoy his time together with Lauren. But he couldn't. Not now. Not when she'd added this new element to their relationship.

"Hey, honey, what's up?" she asked. She shut her door and dropped onto his lap. "Did you hear our show?"

"Yes. What an odd job you have," he said.

"You have no idea. I thought Ray and his producer were going to come to blows. What'd you think?"

He was trying not to. He didn't want to wonder if Lauren had been talking about him today. "It was fun."

"I'm glad you enjoyed it. Why are you here?" she asked.

He cuddled her close, holding her lightly though his gut said to never let her go. But the things he'd always wanted to keep he never could. He flexed his fingers and tried to ignore the fact that Lauren represented many of those "things" he'd always longed for.

"I can't make lunch today," he said. A meeting had come up at work and he couldn't get out of it. The fact that he'd thought about postponing so he could still keep his commitment to Lauren worried him. No woman had ever competed with business before in his eyes.

Was this why his dad's relationships hadn't ever worked out? Because he'd always chosen business over companionship?

"You could have called," she said.

He couldn't read her. Had no idea where they really stood on this. He sucked at relationships with women and wasn't sure why Lauren was so important to him now.

But the last time he'd bungled this relationship thing, he'd hurt her. And he wasn't taking any chances this time. "No, I wanted to make sure there was no misunderstanding."

She punched him lightly on the arm. "Don't say it like I overreacted to a call you made. Last time you didn't call."

He turned his face into her hair so she couldn't see his grin. God, she pleased him on so many levels. It frightened him to think of how deeply he was starting to care for her. "I know. I'm making up for it."

"Yeah?" she asked. There was doubt in her eyes. She'd been hurt by the past, too. He felt like a fool coming here. But when she looked up at him with those wide, honest eyes…

"Yeah," he said. She looked up at him and he caressed the smooth column of her neck. She shivered under his touch and shifted closer to him.

Lust he could understand and justify, but this need

for Lauren went way beyond that. He lowered his head, brushing his lips against her neck. She smelled like flowers and baby shampoo. Nothing seductive in that. But try telling that to his body.

His skin felt too tight and his blood flowed heavier in his veins. She cupped his face in her cold hands and leaned up to kiss him. It was a sweet kiss, but underneath was the passion that flowed so easily between them.

Lauren pulled back and got off his lap. "I have about ten minutes to get back up to promotions for a photo shoot. Is that it?"

"Yeah. I'm leaving my car with you," he said, getting to his feet as well. He tossed his car keys to her.

"Wow, you trust me with your car?" she asked in that sassy way of hers that made him want to put her on her desk and show her who was boss.

"Yes, smart-ass, I am. It's the Porsche." He wasn't sure why. Cars, business—those had always been more important than women. But not Lauren. He refused to analyze it. Knew he'd make a muck of things if he let them get too heavy.

"Why?" she asked, tossing the keys in the air and catching them.

"Because otherwise you won't have a ride home. Can you pick me up later?"

She tilted her head and watched him. He schooled his features to remain bland. But he really wanted to say the hell with everything—his business, hers—and just toss her over his shoulder and take her away.

Her parting words as they'd left her small home early in the morning had played havoc with his concentration all day. He wanted to get them alone and naked so he could explore her limits and if she'd been serious when she said she'd be his slave in the bedroom.

"What are you thinking about? Your pupils are dilated and your skin is flushed."

"Nothing," he said. Damn, even his voice was deeper.

She skimmed her gaze down his body, arching both eyebrows when she noticed the hard-on tenting the front of his pants. "Doesn't look like nothing to me."

"Listen, minx, we both have work to do, so stop trying to tease me or you'll find out just what that gets you."

She licked her lips and came toward him with a slow, measured stride that made her hips sway with each step. "Maybe I like playing with fire."

He should have known better than to tease her. When had Lauren ever reacted the way he'd expected her to?

"One more step and you can say goodbye to your photo shoot."

She didn't hesitate but kept on walking straight toward him, her eyes on his crotch and a smile on her face that said she was more than ready for whatever consequences her actions brought.

* * *

Lauren hadn't meant to start anything sexual here of all places. They were at her work. But she'd always followed the rules before and it had gotten her nowhere. This time she was following her heart.

And it cried out for Jack. She sensed that he was off balance after last night, which she had to admit was so much more than incredible sex. Last night had changed things between them more than she suspected either of them had been ready for.

"Only one step, eh?" she asked. This was what they needed. Mindless sex and flirting. Heartbreak couldn't come of either of those things.

"That's it. Pretend I drew a line right there." He gestured to a spot right in front of her that ran the length of her small office. "And if you cross it…"

"If I cross it…" she said, inching toward that invisible line.

He straightened from where he stood in the doorway, tossed his coat over her guest chair and moved closer to her. "Then the very slippery grasp I have on my control is going to slide away."

"Promise?" she asked. In his eyes she saw the same kind of excitement and desire that burned in her veins.

"Oh, yes. I promise. I'll turn into a raging sex machine."

She started laughing. "I'm going to a judge's ruling on that one. Raging sex machine—that violates all rules of fair play."

"So what's the penalty?" he asked, edging closer to that imaginary line.

She crossed her arms and pretended to think it over. For some reason, being silly with Jack seemed okay. She knew that he respected her and that if she did something totally flirtatious, it was all right with him.

"It's going to be a step one, I'm afraid. I can't allow you to skate on saying something that…"

"Sexy?" he asked, arching one eyebrow at her.

She shook her head, inching closer to him.

"Provocative?" he suggested. Barely any space remained between the two of them. She felt the brush of his breath across her cheek each time he spoke.

The scent of coffee and peppermint wrapped around her. She held one hand up to keep him from coming any closer and to remind him that she was totally in charge.

"You're grasping at straws," she said in her sternest voice.

He canted his body toward her until the tips of her fingers were brushing his cotton button-down shirt. Heat emanated through the cloth. She rubbed her fingers, which were always cold, against him. Slipped her index finger between the buttons and touched his smooth chest. He took a deep breath and his muscles flexed under her touch. She loosened the two buttons on top and bottom of her finger and pushed the shirt open a bit.

"I know. But it's bringing me closer to what I want," he said, his voice a low, husky growl.

"What do you want?" she asked. Teasing aside, she really wanted to know, because he played his own desires like cards held close to his chest. Leaning down, she traced his bared flesh with her tongue. The light dusting of hair on his chest teased her tongue.

"I want you, sweetheart. That's why I'm here in the middle of a business day, playing instead of working," he said, caging her head in his hands, holding her head to his chest. He urged her higher, and she found his flat brown nipple with the tip of her tongue, lapping at him as she would a favorite snack. Last night she hadn't had the time to explore him as she'd wanted to. But today he seemed in no hurry. As though he didn't mind letting her have her way with him.

"Are you going to get into trouble with the boss?" she asked, scraping him with her teeth.

His breath hissed out in a long, low sound. She nibbled her way down his lean abdomen, toward his belt. She'd never felt this kind of freedom with a man. Freedom to explore and do what she wanted.

"I am the boss," he said.

"Not from where I'm standing," Ty said from the doorway.

"Oh, my God." She was going to die of shame. What the hell had she been thinking? Ty was never going to let her live this down. "Make your brother go away."

"Go away, Ty," Jack said, but he kept his hands on her head, holding her close to his chest. She felt cherished and protected by him.

"I can't. I need her upstairs. And I'm paying for every minute you're late, Lauren."

She tried to pull back from Jack, but he held her face tenderly in his hands still. He tipped her head back and lowered his. He kissed her slowly, thoroughly. As if they had all the time in the world and his brother wasn't watching them.

"Don't let Ty embarrass you about this," he said softly. Then, leaning closer, he whispered right in her ear. "You make me wish we were the only ones in the world."

His words warmed her heart and she hugged him close and then stepped away, knowing she had to get back to work and so did he.

"Can I have five more minutes, Ty?"

"Yes, but I'm waiting outside, and if I hear anything that doesn't sound like you getting ready to get back to work…well, I'm calling Mom, Jack, and telling her you have a girlfriend."

"That's real mature," Jack said.

"Ty, please?"

"Five minutes, Lauren."

The door closed quietly and Lauren stared at Jack. She didn't know what to say. She'd never been in this kind of situation before.

His shirt was half-buttoned. He still had a hard-on. She was aroused, and the last thing she wanted to do was pose for a publicity photo.

He buttoned his shirt and then smiled at her.

"We're going to finish this tonight. Do you know where my office is?"

She shook her head. He pulled out a business card and handed it to her. "I'll be ready after six."

She wasn't sure she could wait all day to see him again, she thought as he walked out the door. That scared her, because no man, even the one she'd planned to marry, had ever affected her so deeply.

Ten

Lauren had a lot of time to think after Jack left. Ty didn't say anything as they went upstairs for the photo shoot, but Lauren knew that she'd crossed a line. She was acting out of control. She needed to refocus herself and her energy.

This thing with Jack—she didn't understand it. He wasn't like any man she'd ever dated. A part of her warned that heartache was all that could come of it. He clearly had commitment issues.

He'd told her more than once that he didn't want to be her fairy-tale knight, yet she still tried to see him in that light.

Was she fooling herself? The same way she had

with every man since she'd started dating? She moved away from the group, into the corner, and sank down against the wall. Jack was making her crazy.

He made her feel alive in a way she never had before. She couldn't wait to see him when they were apart. Being together made time stop. She wanted to wallow in that feeling forever.

"You okay?"

Lauren glanced up to see Ray standing there watching her. Rodney, Didi and Ty were clustered around the photographer. Probably all giving him directions on what he was doing wrong.

"Yeah, fine. Just thinking."

"Mind if I join you?" he asked.

"Please do."

Ray sat down next to her. Rubbing the back of his head, he watched Didi with something more than friendly interest. "The show this morning was wild. Do you believe in finding Mr. Right?"

Lauren leaned her head against the wall. That was her problem—believing in things that might not exist. Wanting something that might be part of the modern Hollywood version of the fairy tales she'd been weaned on. Wanting what had been idolized and made into some sort of amalgam that could never really exist in the real world. She wanted that sitcom-perfect relationship that was funny, touching and easily managed in less than thirty minutes each week.

"Sometimes. You?"

He shrugged. "Not so much. I never really put much stock in love and all that."

"Why not?" she asked, because he seemed very alone and not at all happy about it. Plus, she sometimes sensed something between him and Didi—something that said there was more to that relationship than met the eye.

"My career seemed more important," he said.

She didn't think much about her career. She loved her job and liked talking to people. "Our business is hard on marriages. My mom is a television talk-show host, so I know how hard it can be when one spouse is in the spotlight like that." Her dad had always said that he didn't mind his wife's success because he was successful himself. But then, her dad was a wise man who wasn't easily threatened by attacks of the ego.

"Is that why you prefer the night shift?" Ray asked.

She'd never thought about it before. Just knew she liked being on the air at night. The callers were her kind of people. And she'd always felt more alive in the middle of the night. "I guess. More because I don't like a lot of attention. I got into radio because I like music and talking and…well, I wanted to be like my mom."

"I wasn't that close to my parents. Didn't grow up in a loving family. But I can understand that."

She processed what he said. It reminded her a little of Jack's family. She knew his mom had been involved but his dad had been more like…she hated to think it, but she knew from the stories that Ty sometimes told that Diamond Dave had been a bully.

"What about you? Why'd you get into this business?" she asked.

"I got forced into it," he said.

"Like a calling?" she asked, because Ray wasn't the kind of guy she imagined anyone forced to do anything.

"More like a boot to the butt."

Lauren laughed. "I don't understand men."

"What's to understand? Food, sex, sports—life is good."

"If only it were that simple," she said.

"We're ready for you two again," Ty said.

Lauren pushed to her feet and walked back to the photo area. They took their pictures and everyone went back to their offices to take care of the mundane e-mails, calls and paperwork.

The phone rang when she'd finished answering an e-mail from her brother.

"WCPD, this is Lauren."

"Hello, sweetheart."

"You caught me on my way out the door. I might be a few minutes late."

"Ty is a slave master."

"He is not. I was answering some personal e-mails."

"From who?"

"My brother."

"Tell me about him," Jack said.

"He's a big-shot lawyer in Chicago. He's got two kids—they're both hellions like he was. I feel sorry for my sister-in-law."

"You're very familycentric."

She thought about it for a moment. Her family meant everything to her, even when they drove her crazy. "I think that's why I keep looking for that happily ever after. I'm surrounded by examples of how good life can be with the right mate."

Jack didn't respond.

"Jack? You still there?"

He cleared his throat. "Yeah, I'm here."

"What's the matter?" she asked when he still didn't say anything.

"Don't expect too much from me, Lauren," he said.

"I…you've already warned me, remember?"

"Yes, but I got the feeling that you forgot."

She didn't know how to respond to that statement.

"I'll be at your office in twenty minutes," she said, hanging up the phone.

It was true, she was starting to build a pretty little fantasy in her mind that featured her and Jack and a couple of cute little kids. But that wasn't entirely her fault. He kept doing the unexpected—like making her fall in love with him.

Jack looked out the window of his downtown office. He liked his little place in the sky. It was the top floor, the best of the best, and he liked it that way.

He'd had three messages from his dad in the last few days. Jack still put off calling the old man. Dave only called when he wanted to relive his glory days and talk about taking Jack and Ty back out on the road. The Diamond Daredevil's return.

Jack rubbed the back of his neck. Logically he knew that no matter how long or hard he tried to distance himself from his father, there was no escaping the man.

The intercom buzzed and Jack picked it up. It was an archaic system but one his receptionist liked to use. The twenty-year-old was into "retro," or so she said.

"Jack, Lauren is here to pick you up."

"Send her up, Moira."

"Will do, boss man."

Jack left his office and went down the hall to meet the elevator. Lauren emerged a few seconds later. She'd twisted her hair up, and tendrils curled around her face.

"You ready to go?"

"No, but I wanted to meet you."

"Why?"

He'd missed her during the day, but he felt like a sap thinking it, so there was no way in hell he was saying that. He tugged her into his arms. Hugged her close and led her down the hall past the offices of the other executives.

"This is a nice office. Much larger than mine," she said. She paced the room, stopping to look at the pictures and plaques on the wall.

"Thanks." He went back to his desk to finish typing the e-mail he'd been working on. He tried not to notice she was here in the room, but he couldn't help it.

She'd paused in front of a picture of his family taken in 1976. Dave, Ty and Jack all wore American-flag jumpsuits, and his mom stood behind them wearing her red-white-and-blue minidress. That picture had been taken two days before his father's accident.

"I like this photo. You look so young and wild here," she said, reaching out to trace her finger over his image.

Jack sent the e-mail and shut down his computer. He walked over to Lauren. He kept the picture to remind him that life was always full of the unexpected.

"I was wild and a little bit crazy. Kind of like the thing I did with the car that day we went to lunch, except worse," he said. As an adult he'd tried to temper the wildness inside him, sensing that it could be his undoing, much the same as it had been his dad's. But there were times and people who made his control threadbare. Lauren was one of those people.

Around her he simply reacted instead of thinking. Logic flew out the window and lust rippled to life. He wanted to do crazy things that would impress her. Anything that showed her he was the best man in the world for her.

But inside he wasn't sure he was the best man for Lauren.

"Like what?" she asked. She tucked a strand of her dark hair behind her ear.

He shrugged off his thoughts of the present and tried to remember something tame that he could tell her about his childhood. Something that wouldn't make her look at him as if he was a little insane. But his father hadn't been like other dads, and impressing the old man had called for outrageous stunts. "Like riding my bike off the roof."

"Oh, my God." She reached over and grabbed his wrist. He felt a faint trembling in her fingers. "Did you break an arm or a leg? Duke did that one time when he was eight."

He shook his head. "I've always known how to take a fall. So I was pretty loose when I came off the bike. I sprained my wrist, but that was all."

She didn't let go of him but continued caressing the underside of his wrist. He tried—really tried—to keep his mind on what she was saying, but his body was reacting to her touch and her nearness.

"Did you get in trouble?" she asked.

He pulled away from her. He shouldn't have mentioned the past. Unlike Lauren and her warm family unit, his family had been different. Focused on other things—like winning, staying out of his dad's way and never showing a weakness.

"Oh, yes. I wrecked the bike, one of my dad's motocross ones. He was livid." Jack could still see the anger in his father's face. It was the first time he'd seen that much emotion out of the old man that wasn't swaggering pride. At first, Jack had thought his father was concerned about Jack's health. But that had quickly changed.

"Oh, Jack," she said so softly he had to strain to hear her.

"Don't say it like that, Lauren. I was old enough to know better than to take my dad's stuff without permission."

She nodded. "I can say it however I like. You were a kid trying to be like his dad. He should have patted you on the back and—"

"He should have told me I was crazy. Nobody should ride a bike off their roof."

Wrapping her arm around his waist, she leaned her head against his chest. "You're right. But in your family it's kind of a tradition."

He rubbed her back and struggled against the feelings that were swirling inside him. Lauren was the first one to ever take his side in this debate. And it had been going on for years. Even Ty sided with his dad.

But Lauren wasn't objective or impartial and she'd understood, without him having to say a word, what he'd wanted. He resented that she knew him so well. Was he so transparent?

Lauren wasn't sure what to do. Jack held her loosely in his arms, but she knew he felt anything but relaxed. There was a tension in him that surrounded her.

"How'd you like driving the Porsche?" he asked. He rubbed his jaw against the top of her head.

She forced herself not to hold him too tightly. His deep voice was soothing after the long day, and she knew she wanted to come home to him for the rest of her life. Sometimes he was so tender—it was almost as if he cherished her. And that was really what she'd been searching for.

"I was scared the entire time I'd wreck it," she said carefully.

He pulled back, tipped her chin up. "Did you?"

He didn't look or sound worried, but she knew that car was one of his prized possessions. Even if she hadn't seen the way he babied it with his car cover. Ty's reaction when he'd realized Jack was letting her drive the car had been a dead giveaway. "What do you think?"

"That you're a firecracker and a half. But a safe driver."

She was a rule follower, which was why it had always bothered her that she hadn't found a mate. She'd been doing everything a woman in the new century was supposed to do, but here she was, still alone.

"You're right, I am. I was tempted to take the interstate out of the city and find some nice deserted country road, but then I thought of you trapped here in the office all night."

He gave her a quick squeeze before letting her go. He looked devastatingly handsome in his suit. But then, he had a gorgeous bod and looked good in anything—or nothing.

"Are you free this weekend?" he asked.

"Yes. Why?" Did he want to plan a trip? All of her doubts about Jack and that damned playboy reputation of his were slowly being laid to rest.

"Want to take the car on a road trip?" he asked. He moved around the office, turning off lights, shutting the shades and straightening the papers in his in-box.

She couldn't read his features and see what his reaction was. She moved closer, but when he looked up at her, she still couldn't read anything in his face.

"Do you want to think about it overnight?"

She didn't have to think about it. She wanted to spend all her weekends with Jack. But she was trying to find some sort of compromise between who she was and who she wanted Jack to see. "No, I don't need to think about it, Jack. I'd love to take a road trip this weekend."

He nodded, but she noticed his shoulders relaxed. What kind of traveler was he? She was a talker. What if she annoyed him before they reached the city limits of Detroit?

"Good. We can drive down to Chicago, stay on Michigan Avenue. Eat and shop to our heart's content."

Forgetting for a moment that he'd said "shop," which was one of her favorite pastimes—ugh, not her hometown. Not the bastion of the Belchoir clan. "No. Not Chicago. I can't sneak into the city where my family is and not get caught."

He slipped his hand under her elbow, leading her

out of his office and into the hallway. "Who said you had to sneak?"

"You want to meet them?" she asked while he locked his door and left a sheaf of papers on his secretary's desk.

"Sure. Why wouldn't I?"

Her family was lovable and nice. Most people liked them—but Lauren's boyfriends often didn't. She was the baby of her family and really couldn't explain it to anyone who wasn't also the youngest, but they treated her as if she needed protecting. They treated any man she brought home to the third degree. They'd treat him like someone they wanted their daughter to marry, and Jack had said he wasn't ready for that.

And she wasn't ready to let him go. Not this soon. She was still trying to figure out how to keep him forever without spooking him.

"Lauren?"

Too much time had passed. He was going to think something was wrong.

She hit the call button for the elevator and tried to sound nonchalant. "If you do meet the entire family and they like you, I'm going to start having those uncontrollable fantasies that you're my Mr. Right again."

The elevator car arrived and he motioned for her to enter. Maybe they could drop the subject. She'd find a nice B and B somewhere in a neighboring city.

Maybe someplace secluded in the Upper Peninsula for the weekend. That would be a lot easier on both of them.

He shrugged and pulled her closer by the lapels of her coat.

She leaned into his body. She liked the way he felt against her. Leaning down, he brushed his lips over hers in a way that she was beginning to get addicted to. "Open for me. It's been too long since I tasted you."

She opened her mouth and he slid his tongue inside with a long, languid stroke. The embrace was slow and easy and felt intimate and familiar. She hugged him closer. Tipped her head back farther, inviting him deeper.

His hands slid up and he held her head, his fingers massaging the back of her neck. She loved the way he enfolded her in intimacy. Made her feel as if the rest of the world didn't exist.

The elevator door *bing*ed and opened on the ground floor. Jack stepped back slowly, dropping a few nibbling kisses on her lips before stepping out of the elevator.

The snow fell steadily while they were inside. It coated the ground and the car, which sat out front where she'd parked it in the spot with his name on it.

She shook her head as he seated her in the car. But there was a warm feeling growing between them, and for the first time in a relationship Lauren felt as if this might really be the real thing.

Eleven

Lauren said little more about visiting Chicago over the weekend. Jack let it go. It had been a long day at work, so he suggested stopping to eat dinner at his favorite sushi bar.

Oslo was located in the downtown area, just off Woodward. The hostess recognized Jack and they were seated immediately. "This isn't like any sushi bar I've ever been in."

"I know. The owner prides himself on being different."

Jack told himself he'd stopped here because Lauren would like it and it was a nice place to eat, but he knew he was avoiding taking her to his home, where he wanted to keep her. Avoiding continuing down the emotional path that he was still busy denying existed between them. Avoiding anything that resembled what he wanted so much.

Because that picture in his office of his family had reminded Jack of things Lauren made him want to forget—family and happily ever after were elusive. Jack was enough of his father's son to believe that once you found that kind of happiness, you weren't allowed to keep it.

Maybe that was why he wanted to go to Chicago with her. To see if that kind of bond really did last or if her parents had turned into some kind of bored-with-each-other married couple.

"You're frowning," she said, interrupting his thoughts. She leaned across the table and took his hand in both of hers. Her fingers were cold, as always, and he brought his other hand up to cup hers.

She smiled absently as he rubbed her fingers.

"I am?" he asked.

"You were. What were you thinking about?"

"Nothing important."

"Your dad?" she asked.

It scared him how intuitive she was to his feelings. He'd made a vow long ago to be a loner. Not because he wanted to be alone but because it was safer that way. Safer for him. He'd always craved the kind of intimacy that Lauren wove so effortlessly around the two of them.

"No," he said.

"Uh-oh, you're frowning again. Have you decided you don't want sushi?" she asked.

He knew she was deliberately changing the subject. And though he was glad to change it, another part of him resented the fact that she was managing him. Doing what she needed to keep him happy. Dammit, he wanted to be the one who took care of her.

"Never. It's my favorite." He was determined to shake off his mood and make this date one she'd remember. They should have gotten takeout. Then they'd be back at his place and he could make love to her. Truthfully it was the only time he felt in control around her—when they were lying naked with each other and he was deep inside her body.

She made a silly face at him, and he realized that Lauren was completely comfortable with him. She wasn't pretending to be someone she wasn't. Just baring her soul and her vulnerabilities to him. He wanted to warn her that he couldn't do that. Wouldn't be the kind of man who could open his soul up to her.

"Say what you will, but my dad is a country boy and he always calls sushi 'bait with rice,'" she said in a teasing tone.

"I can see why you'd be reluctant to eat it," he said. The more he thought about it, he had kind of said "Let's stop for sushi" instead of asking her what she wanted. "Do you want to eat here or did you just agree to make me happy?"

Tipping her head to the side, she looked at him for a long moment. All her emotions were there in her gaze, and he felt so unworthy of that kind of trust and caring.

"I love miso soup. I never would have tried this place if you hadn't suggested it."

"We can go somewhere else," he said. He had to get her out of here. This was a big mistake. Letting her get so close. He could never protect her.

Suddenly he realized that was exactly what he wanted to do. He'd been hurt before and he wasn't looking to be hurt again, but that mattered little compared to Lauren's feelings. Hell, he was falling in love with her.

"No. Really, I was just making conversation, not complaining. Sorry." Her fingers tightened on his and he saw the anxiety in her eyes. The worry that she'd done something wrong.

"No problem."

She let go of his hands and picked up her menu. He felt her pulling back and knew he was responsible for it. He thought about ignoring the entire thing, pretending he didn't know that he'd hurt her feelings, but in the end he couldn't.

"I told you I'm still mostly a frog," he said softly.

"No, you're not. It's just more convenient for you to be one."

"That might be true. We all have walls to hide behind. Even you," he said. She'd been the one who

didn't want to go visit her family this weekend. And
he knew that he'd pushed hard to see her reaction to
taking him home.

"Yes, but I'm willing to try. I'm willing to risk it all."

He realized that she was, and that was what really
scared him. Because he didn't want her to risk it all
on him and find out that he was really just a frog underneath all the outward trappings of a successful man.

It was almost nine o'clock when they finished eating, and Lauren suggested they go back to her place.
She had to get up early for work the next day.

"Come stay with me tonight. I want you in my
bed," Jack said.

Who could resist that? They stopped by her place
and she got her car and a change of clothes. Lauren
pulled into his driveway and turned off her car.

It felt like coming home, especially when Jack
opened her door and led her into the house. He scooped
her up in his arms and carried her back to his bedroom.

"The first night we went snowshoeing, this is what
I wanted," he said, setting her in the center of his bed.
He toed off his shoes, shed his tie and socks and then
started unbuttoning his shirt.

Lauren just enjoyed watching him strip for her.
His body was masculine perfection. He dropped his
shirt to the floor and unfastened his belt.

"Me, too. But I was trying to make sure you'd respect me," she said.

"I have nothing but respect for a woman who knows what she wants. Aren't you going to take off your clothes?" he asked. His belt was gone and he unfastened his pants.

"I definitely know what I want," she said. Sitting, she unzipped her boots and tossed them on the floor. Then pulled off her socks. Her sweater went over her head and landed on the floor at his feet.

"Hmm?" He pushed his underwear down his legs with his pants and stood before her, naked and ready.

"You," she said, shivering with desire. Her fingers fumbled with the fastening of her pants and finally she had them undone. She shoved them down her legs and kicked them aside as Jack crouched on the end of the bed.

"Don't take off anything else."

She only had on her matching ice-blue bra-and-panties set. She liked the bra because it was one of those that made her look as if she had real cleavage. The cups were made of satin and a thin layer of lace.

Jack took her ankles in his hands and tugged gently until she was lying on her back. He pushed her legs apart until there was ample room to accommodate him.

"That's better."

He kissed and nibbled his way up one leg. Slowly he reached her inner thigh. Her nipples tightened and her breasts felt full. She canted her hips toward his mouth and his warm breath. But he put his hands on her waist, holding her still.

"Not yet," he murmured against her skin.

She shook at the feeling of that warm breath against the joint of her leg. He licked her carefully there and then breathed heavily over her satin-covered mound. She whimpered as he brushed his fingers in a featherlight stroke over her.

"Too much?"

"Yes. Jack, I need you."

"Just a little longer. Anticipation makes everything better."

He traced his tongue down the center of her satin panties and she groaned his name. He did that three times before she reached down and tunneled her fingers through his hair, holding him to her.

He used his teeth to peel her underwear down, revealing her to him. But he tugged them only as far as the top of her thighs and left them there. He came back to her, parting her with his thumbs and using his tongue and fingers to arouse her.

She was on the edge and couldn't take much more. He pushed two fingers into her sheath and continued to suckle at her most delicate flesh. Her hips strained up against his mouth. Her hands caught at his head and shoulders as her body climbed frantically toward orgasm. It rippled over her and she called his name.

Jack slid up her body, holding her close until the tremors passed. Then he pushed her underwear down her legs and lowered his mouth to her stomach. He teased her belly button and traced the line of her ribs with his tongue.

He used his fingers to peel back the lace on her bra. She felt his breath on her nipple before his tongue traced over her. Her hips lifted and she felt his erection so close to her center. She slid her hands down his body to touch him there and felt wetness on the tip.

She stroked that liquid down his length and heard him groan softly as she reached between his legs to cup his sac.

He closed his mouth over her nipple and suckled as she continued to fondle him. He grew longer and harder against her. Lauren felt a moment of female power at her ability to arouse Jack like this.

She wanted to play his game, to draw this out between them until he couldn't think, the way he had to her. But more than anything she just wanted him to slide home. She needed to feel his slim hips between her legs. His hard erection buried inside her. His seed spilling deep in her.

She scraped her nails up his back and pulled his head up. He leaned up until he could kiss her. As his body moved over hers, caressing her everywhere. His hardness nudged between her legs, rubbing over her very sensitive flesh.

His chest brushed over the tips of her breasts, the light dusting of hair teasing her responsive nipples.

His whole body made love to hers and she

couldn't wait another minute. She reached between them, grasping him and directing him toward her center.

"No more waiting. I need you," she said, her words deep and husky.

His eyes narrowed and he pulled back. He grabbed a pillow from the head of the bed and shoved it under her hips, canting her body for his entry. He held her still and looked into her eyes, and Lauren thought she saw his soul reflected there.

She felt the tip of his body at her entrance. But he stopped again, waiting. "Jack, take me now."

"Watch me," he said, his voice more of a grunt. "Watch me take you."

She nodded and looked down their bodies to the part where they were almost joined. He entered her slowly and she watched as he penetrated her body, making her his.

He kept his thrusts strong and sure, and Lauren felt everything in her body start to tighten with the approach of her climax. She lifted her eyes and met Jack's. "I'm coming."

"Not yet," he said, lowering himself on top of her and continuing to thrust. "Together."

He slid his hands up her body, linked their fingers together, stretching her arms over her head as he increased the tempo of his thrusts. He lowered his head to her breast and suckled. She was so close; she knew she was going to…

"Jack?"

"Now," he said against her nipple. She felt him spill his seed deep inside her as her body rippled into orgasm, clenching around his penis. She shivered and shook as he continued to thrust until his body was completely empty.

She slipped her arms around him and held him tight, knowing she'd found the man she'd always been searching for. "I love you."

He rolled them both to their sides and then pulled the end of the comforter over them.

He made love to her again and Lauren fell into an exhausted sleep. Only just before the alarm rang did she realize that Jack had never said he loved her back.

Panic unlike anything Jack had ever felt before seized him. He knew that Lauren was going to slip through his fingers. Hadn't she realized anything he'd shown her? Didn't she understand he wasn't a man to reveal something like that?

He felt her watching him as the alarm rang. Felt her eyes on him, and the weight of those words he hadn't said fell heavily on his shoulders. But he wasn't going to say them. Wasn't even sure he felt them. What the hell did a man like him know about love?

Why the hell did she think he could be her white knight? Hadn't he shown her he was really just a frog?

Because he couldn't—wouldn't—say the words

she needed to hear, he showed her in the only way he was really comfortable what she meant to him.

She meant more to him than any other person. They'd slept spooned together, and his morning erection nudged at the heat between her legs. He wanted her again. He'd never be able to get enough of her and yet he knew this was the last time he'd make love to her.

He knew after this morning, once Lauren got out of his bed, things would change. Either she'd bring up the subject of love again or she'd ignore it. God, please let her ignore it.

He didn't want to see hurt in her big, expressive eyes.

He skimmed his hands down her soft body, still warm with sleep. He urged her forward until she was on her stomach. He hadn't had the time last night to finish exploring her body and to find out how she responded everywhere.

It was too soon to be the end. He wasn't ready to give her up. Later he could debate the wisdom of allowing three little words to have such power over him. But right now he needed her. He needed to feel the velvet warmth of her body squeezing around him one last time.

He reached over and switched on the lamp on the nightstand. Lauren turned her head on the pillow and rolled over. He met her gaze. There was a sadness in her eyes that cut him deep.

He couldn't make this right. Maybe he should just get her out of his bed. But he wasn't ready to let go yet. Would he ever be freaking ready to let this woman go?

His heart said no but his weary soul said he had to. He leaned down to kiss her carefully, keeping his eyes closed so he wouldn't see the hurt in her eyes. She made that sound deep in her throat that made him want to come.

Turning her body more fully into his, she wrapped her leg over his hip. He'd wanted to make love to her one last time in a way he wouldn't have to see her face or her eyes, but he realized that Lauren had different plans.

She, too, sensed this was their last time, and he felt in her the need to leave her mark on him. Didn't she realize she'd already marked his soul?

She pushed him onto his back, kneeling by his side. She leaned over him, teasing his flat nipples with her tongue and teeth. She played her fingers down his body, stroking over his ribs, tracing the line of hair that ran down his center.

Every inch of his body was sensitized to her touch. He was rock-hard and wanted to be inside her now. Enough teasing. He grabbed her by her waist and lifted her over him.

She sat up and he could feel the creamy warmth of her center on his hard-on. She straddled him, rubbed her breasts against his chest and then reached between them to take his erection, leading him to her entrance.

She impaled herself on him slowly, sinking back on her heels. She stopped once she was fully seated. "Did you watch me take you, Jack?"

He realized he had.

"You're mine."

He wrapped his arms around her, pulling her torso down to his, and rolled them over. It was an awkward move, but he managed to stay inside her body until she was beneath him. He held her hips and thrust into her body.

"No," he said, his own voice heavy with arousal and another emotion only he knew was fear. *"You are mine."*

He watched her eyes widen, and she held tight to his shoulders, her fingernails sinking into his back as he rode her harder and deeper than he had the night before, taking them both more quickly to the pinnacle.

She shuddered in his arms, and a second later he spilled himself inside her. As quickly as the storm had built between them, it ebbed, leaving Jack feeling weak.

He lowered his head, pillowing himself on her sweet breasts while she stroked his back.

Her body still contracted around him and her hips thrust upward every few seconds. The moment was almost sweet. The only thing missing were those few words that he needed to say.

She held him so tenderly. No other woman ever had just offered him the comfort of her body. The ease of her soul and that quiet understanding of his faults.

She was offering him whatever peace he needed to finally say the words she needed to hear. But it wasn't enough for him.

As the silence lengthened, he realized she felt their absence, as well. Her fingers stopped moving on his back and she pushed at his shoulders.

"I need to get ready for work."

Jack rolled over and let her go, feeling more of a bastard in this moment than in any other. But he couldn't change a lifetime worth of behavior in such a short amount of time. His entire life had taught him that love at first sight never lasted. No matter what his lonely soul cried for, Jack Montrose knew better than to believe in the love that Lauren had for him.

Because if he did and she left him, he'd be even lonelier than he had been before he met her.

Twelve

"**G**ood morning, listeners. This is Lauren B. and Ray King telling you there are only two days left to sign up for the Mile of Men competition," Lauren said.

"That's right, listeners, it's not too late to participate and find a date for Valentine's Day," Ray said.

Lauren was too tired this morning. Her heart was heavy and she knew that Jack was to blame. She had no idea what to do to get through to him. What was her problem when it came to men? The thing was, with Jack she knew she'd found the kind of man who'd be perfect for a happily-ever-after scenario if he'd just let himself be happy.

"Lauren?"

"Sorry, Ray. I'm distracted this morning, listeners. Having a little trouble with the entire dating scene."

"Wanna talk about it?" Ray asked, waggling his eyebrows at her. "What do you say, listeners? Are you ready to help Lauren out this morning?"

For a minute she didn't want to. She knew how Jack felt about being in the spotlight but felt confident that no one really knew who she was dating, save Ty. She didn't know if this was a good idea. Jack wasn't like all the other men she'd dated.

But it was too late and Lauren knew better than to try to get out of this on the air. She'd talk to Ray later and warn him to not jump into these sorts of situations in the future.

"Yes, I think I do. Here's the situation. The guy can't commit. I think he'd be happy to leave things the way they are right now but I…I feel like he's the one. So what do I do?"

The call lines lit up. Ray talked them into a commercial break while Didi and Rodney screened the callers. Rodney flashed her a message on her computer screen. *Jack, line three—not happy.*

Lauren picked up the line. "Jack?"

"What are you doing? You can't talk about our problems—"

"No one knows they're our problems. They don't even know your name. Trust me, Jack. You're perfectly safe in your penthouse office, with your rotating cars and your ever-changing world."

He cursed under his breath. She heard the static and knew he was on his cell phone. It was only seven-thirty, and she knew he normally didn't leave his house until eight o'clock to get to work.

"This isn't about you anymore," she said softly. She wished it was. But keeping it private hadn't worked for her. It never did. Why did she keep trying to find love when she knew…

What did she know?

"Hell yes, it is about you and I. And I can understand why you're doing it," he said.

She heard the pain in his voice and wanted to comfort him. A big part of her wanted to bury her own feelings and not rock the boat. Yet another deeper part of her understood that with Jack that would be the end of her. He was the man of her dreams, and if he wasn't going to be there for the long haul, she needed to get out now.

"Why?" she asked.

"You're just like me when it comes to intimacy."

That hurt. But then, the truth always did. She knew that Jack was striking back, cleverly pointing out that he wasn't the only one who bore the blame for their problem. "No I'm not. I told you how I feel."

"Touché. But talking about your problems on the air with faceless listeners—that's not a real connection, Lauren."

"I wanted to talk to you," she said. And she'd tried, but he'd hurried her out the door this morning.

"I'm sorry."

There was pain in his voice and it went straight to her heart. "I don't need you to say something you don't feel. I just need to know…that you're not pushing me away."

"Back in five seconds, Lauren."

"I have to work. Can you hold?"

"Dammit. Yes."

She typed a message to Rodney telling him to leave Jack's call on three, and then they were back on the air.

"I had the same problem with a guy I dated for six months. He was everything I wanted in a man, but when that time was up he…he ended things. Told me his life worked in cycles and the one that featured the two of us was ending."

The words and actions sounded so familiar. "What was his name?"

"Jack."

Lauren couldn't listen anymore. Didn't want to hear what she'd known in her heart. He wasn't her dream man. He was every woman's dream man, going through the motions of creating a perfect little relationship. And that was how he existed. He filled his life with these pockets of time. These picture-perfect relationships that never lasted.

"What happened? Did you find love later?"

"Yes. It wasn't that kind of perfect fairy-tale version of love and life together, but I'm content now."

They took two more callers, and luckily neither of

them had been involved with Jack. But Lauren wasn't paying attention anymore. Was she expecting something that was unrealistic with Jack?

They went to another commercial break. The light on three was still flashing so she pressed the button. "Are you still there?"

"Yes. I know what you're thinking."

"I doubt that."

"Dammit, Lauren, you mean more to me than any other woman ever has. Can't that be enough?"

She started to say yes, but she thought about the woman caller who'd found happiness without the trimmings. She thought about the people who went on her mother's show who struggled to find contentment in the real world.

She thought about her sister-in-law who said marriage isn't about romance and flowers but about finding someone you can tolerate day in and day out. And her dreams slowly died. For real this time. She knew that she was chasing after something with Jack that wasn't going to happen.

"Sure, Jack. That can be enough. Enough for how long—five and a half more months?"

"Dammit, Lauren—"

"Yes, dammit, Jack." She disconnected the call. She knew that Jack had touched her soul. That finding this kind of love and the connection that was between them was once in a lifetime, and it broke her heart that he didn't recognize that, as well.

* * *

Lauren wasn't answering his calls, and Jack had endured a lecture from his secretary on his bad mood. He didn't care. He knew he'd lost Lauren and he was trying to come to terms with it but he wasn't ready to let her go.

Leaving her after six months would have been a struggle because he knew he loved her. But he refused to let himself be vulnerable like that. Every time his mom had fallen in love, a few weeks later her man would leave.

Jack's dad's relationships had been little better. But he didn't know how to change things.

Ty called just after seven o'clock and invited Jack to join his weekly poker match. The last thing Jack wanted to do was be around other people, but Ty was adamant. So twenty minutes later he found himself sitting in Ty's poker room, smoking a cigar and hitting the scotch a little too heavily.

Ty's best friend, Bert, was there, as well as the new morning DJ, Ray King. Bert and Ty had been friends since the third grade, so he was like a little brother to Jack. But the DJ was a stranger, and Jack knew he was going to have to temper his mood.

But he didn't want to. He'd spent most of his life pretending he wasn't wild like Diamond Dave, pretending he was sleek and sophisticated, a *GQ* kind of guy, when he knew he was just a crazy stuntman like his dad who lived life best at ninety miles an hour.

Finally Jack understood why his dad never slowed down. You didn't see the roadkill at ninety miles an hour. People that you hurt blended into the past, and the new road was there ahead, beckoning with its sweet promise of… What the hell did it promise? He wasn't sure anymore. But he knew it was a promise bathed in acceptance and without the kind of pain he felt right now.

Ray eyed him speculatively.

"You okay, *compare?*"

"Yeah."

"It's not too late to sign up for the Mile of Men."

"Forget it. I don't do those kinds of publicity stunts," Jack said, realizing he was looking for a fight. Probably not a good idea at his brother's house. With one of his brother's employees.

Jack kept to himself after that, downing glass after glass of scotch and pretending that he was fooling Ty and the others into believing he was okay.

"Go easy on the liquor, Jack," Ty said.

"Leave me alone, little brother, unless you want to take this discussion outside." He was just drunk enough to know that fighting with Ty wasn't what he really wanted to do. A few more glasses and it wouldn't matter, but right now it still did. Jack lowered his glass to the table and concentrated instead on his cards.

"Oh, ho. I think Ty can take you in this condition," Bert said.

Maybe. But Jack felt mean deep inside and he

knew he wouldn't fight fair. Wouldn't remember that Ty was his brother and didn't deserve the fight Jack wanted.

"Women problems, *compare?*" Ray asked.

"Yes. But I already heard it discussed on your show this morning."

"So you're the one?" Ray asked.

Jack reached for his glass and emptied it in one long swallow. He shrugged at Ray. The older man had a shrewd glance that made Jack feel as if Ray knew what he was hiding. Understood that Jack wasn't ready to let go of Lauren but also felt he had no real right to hold on to her.

"Damn, Jack. Your woman talked about you on the air?" Bert took a sip of his Corona, leaning back in his chair.

"Don't push, Bert. I'm looking for a fight."

"Hell, we can all see that," Ty said. "Help me out in the kitchen, Jack."

Since he was losing anyway, Jack threw his cards on the table, grabbed the bottle of scotch and followed Ty into his kitchen.

"What the hell is going on?" Ty asked.

"None of your business," Jack said.

"Oh, but it is. I gave Lauren your number. I feel responsible."

"Don't, Ty. I'm the older one. I take care of our problems."

"I don't think you can anymore, Jack. What's

wrong? Lauren's not like the other women you've dated. She's real. You know what I mean? Real in a way that our lives never have been."

"You think I don't know that? Hell, that's why I'm backing off. What do I know about making a relationship last?"

"I don't know, bro. But I do know that you've been different since Lauren came into your life. I think…hell, who am I to give advice. But I really think that if you can let go of the past, you could be happy with her."

Jack said nothing. But he heard the truth in Ty's words. And a part of him wanted to believe it. "Remember the Fourth when I was eight and you were five? Remember how perfect everything was that day? Dad jumped—what?—eight cars. Mom made cookies that didn't burn. And you and I, we were kings at that festival. Remember?"

"Yeah," Ty said.

Jack leaned against the countertop, remembering how perfect everything had been. Their family had seemed like…he couldn't explain it, but everything had been just right. For the first time there had been no fighting between his parents.

And Jack had believed the way only an eight-year-old could that things were okay. That his family was going to be one of the families that others envied.

"Then two damned days later it all fell apart," Jack said more to himself than to Ty.

"But with Lauren it'll be different."

Jack heard the hope in his brother's voice and knew it was one he foolishly shared.

"I can't take a chance on being wrong, Ty. I don't want to hurt her like that."

Jack pushed past his brother and walked outside in the bracing chilly air of February. But he didn't feel it. He'd already hardened his heart and wrapped it in ice. Nothing could compare to the iciness he felt now that he was alone again.

The door opened behind Jack and he glanced over to see Ray. Jack remembered the first day he'd met the older man. It was the same day he'd met Lauren. He barely remembered anything that he'd said to her that day. But the sound of her voice still echoed in his mind. How it had stroked down his spine and kindled a longing to get to know all her secrets.

"Wanna talk about your problems?" Ray asked. He took a puff on his cigar and crossed his arms over his rounded belly. Ray looked like a gangster, a Tony Soprano kind of guy, and just the thought of confessing to him made Jack want to laugh.

"No. I'm not a touchy-feely kind of guy when it comes to my emotions."

Ray shrugged and leaned forward, bracing his hands on the railing, looking out into the night as if he were searching for some kind of answer in the sky. "Me either. But women sure are."

"You got problems?" Jack asked. *Thank God.* He was tired of feeling like the only man who was dealing with weighty issues. What was weighty? He was in love with a woman and afraid to take a chance that his emotions might be real. Afraid to risk himself for her. And he knew that was the real heart of his problems.

"Not really. But I got this broad that keeps making me wish things were different, ya know?"

"Yeah, I do."

Ray leaned against the railing, the stub of the cigar between his teeth, watching Jack with a shrewd gaze. Jack wished he hadn't had that last glass of scotch. Things were a little hazy, and he wasn't going to be able to drive home.

Maybe he'd call Lauren and ask her to come pick him up. The hell of it was, he knew she would do it. That despite the fact that he'd acted like an ass earlier, she'd come and get him. But he knew it was the same thing she'd do for any of her friends.

"Just go to her and talk to her. Women understand that kind of thing."

Jack thought he was hearing things, then realized that Ray had spoken. He shook his head. This had been a mistake. He was going to call Carl and then go home to sleep off the liquor, and in the morning he was booking himself on the first flight to somewhere warm. He wasn't coming home until after Valentine's Day. After he'd forgotten about Lauren. After she'd had a chance to move on.

"I can't. She deserves better." And she did. She deserved a real white knight. A real Prince Charming who wasn't just a frog underneath. Jack took a step off the porch, but Ray grabbed his shoulder and stopped him.

"I'm not really a DJ," Ray said.

"Whatever, man, let go." Jack shrugged off Ray's grip but the man held tight.

"I'm a matchmaker."

"I think I had a little too much to drink," Jack muttered.

"Hell, believe me, I wish it was the liquor, but the truth is, I'm here to make sure you don't screw things up with Lauren."

"I'd like to believe you, Ray, really I would. But why are you here now?"

"There's no rhyme or reason to this thing. *Madon'*, I keep trying to figure out the rules, but when Didi sends me to help someone…"

"Your producer is in on the matchmaking thing, too? How much did you have to drink tonight?"

"Not enough," Ray said. "*Madon',* why can't this ever be easy?"

Jack felt as if he was moving, and the next instant he was standing inside the radio booth. A pregnant Lauren was working, headphones on, playing that sexy music of hers and laughing as she had a quiet conversation with a man.

"Where the hell are we?"

"The future."

"So it works out with Lauren and…"

"A guy named Paul."

Jack felt a stabbing pain in his stomach. Lauren looked happy. Was she really happy? He moved closer to her.

"Can she see me?"

"Uh, no. We're just here to observe."

Jack didn't stop until he was close enough that her scent wrapped around him. He lowered his head to the top of her curly hair. At least she was happy. That's what he wanted, he realized—Lauren to be happy.

Closing his eyes, he listened to her speaking. She was on the line but not on the air.

"Sure, Paul. You can come home tonight."

"I'm sorry, babe. It didn't mean anything. It's just that you can't have sex right now."

Lauren rubbed her forehead. "That's okay."

Hell, no it wasn't. Why would she allow herself to be treated like that?

"What's going on here, Ray? She's supposed to be happy."

"She settled for safe," Ray said.

"This is wrong," Jack said.

"Yes it is. She belongs with you."

Jack's hands were shaking. Suddenly he was

standing outside alone on Ty's porch. He sank to the bottom step and stared up at the stars.

He was having one bad trip. He didn't want to see Lauren crying. He didn't want to see Lauren pregnant with anyone's child but his. He didn't want to spend the rest of his life alone without the woman he loved.

He thought about his life. About changing. Leaving behind his new apartment and keeping one car for longer than six months. He thought about waking up with Lauren every day, and a feeling almost like peace spread through him.

Oh, God, nothing scared him more than having to talk to her. To tell her how he felt and acknowledge that he was going to try to be that white knight she'd always dreamed of.

Hell, he had no idea how to even get her to believe him.

Thirteen

Lauren had spent the weekend in Chicago with her family. After having her heart broken, she'd needed to go someplace where she was loved and spoiled. Her mother had danced around the subject and Lauren had realized she wasn't solving anything by running away.

She'd returned to Detroit early Monday morning, going straight to work. It was the day of the Mile of Men, and as soon as they got off the air she was going to confront Jack and make him realize what he was throwing away.

Ray was in early. They were doing a remote broadcast from the revitalized Fox Theatre on Woodward Avenue. The lobby was full of the men who'd signed up to be a part of the mile.

Since it was February and very cold outside, they had runners who were taking hot drinks to the men and making sure no one stayed outside for too long. They'd set up warming stations on every block and rotated the men in and out of the heated tents.

Seeing so many people taking a chance on love, searching for the same things she'd always been searching for, made it easier to accept the decision she'd made on the long drive back to Detroit.

Jack might think he couldn't be her white knight, but she was going to convince him that he already was. The white knight didn't have to be perfect.

"Caller, you're on the air."

"One of the men isn't playing fair."

"What do you mean?"

"He's on the side of the road, but instead of a number he's wearing a big red heart with a name on it."

"Whose name?" Lauren asked. This was interesting.

"I couldn't read it. But I thought only available men were supposed to be out there."

"They are," Ray said. "Lauren will go check the guy out and pull him from the line."

"I will?" Lauren asked.

"Yes. I'm not going out on such a cold morning."

"There it is, friends, Ray King is a creature of his own comfort."

Ray winked at her, and Lauren left the broadcast

booth and went out to find the guy who was already in love with a woman. Poor man. He was probably one of those saps who put up billboards declaring their love to a woman because he was afraid to talk to her.

A small crowd had gathered around the man, and as Lauren pushed her way through the crowd, she recognized the camel-colored wool coat that he wore. Recognized the way his hair brushed his collar. Recognized the way he held himself with too much confidence.

"Jack?"

He turned to face her, and she saw in his eyes the truth before she skimmed her gaze down his chest and saw that big red heart with her name on it.

He pushed his way through the people around him and swept her up in his arms. He buried his face against her neck, holding her so tightly that she knew in her heart he was never letting her go.

"I'm so sorry. I know I'm going to screw up. Hell, I'm probably never going to be the man of your dreams, but I can't let you go."

"You already are the man of my dreams," she said.

He cupped her face in his hands, rubbing his thumb over her lower lip. "Don't settle, Lauren. Don't accept less than you deserve. Make me be the man you need."

"I don't have to make you, Jack. You're the only one who sees a frog. I've always seen my Prince Charming. But you were running too fast to notice."

"I'm not running now, sweetheart. I'm standing still and I need you by my side."

Her heart was beating too fast and tears burned the backs of her eyes as he lowered his head. He rubbed his mouth against hers and kissed her with a fierceness she recognized deep in her soul.

That kiss said the things she wanted to hear and would make him confess later when they were alone. She tasted his hope for the future, his fears of the unknown and his promises to her.

When he lifted his head, she hugged him tight to her, resting her head right over his heart.

He leaned down and spoke right into her ear. "I love you, Lauren. And that scares me."

She nodded. She understood fear. She took his hand and led him across the street to the small diner where they'd had coffee that first night. The place wasn't too crowded. They found a booth at the back and Lauren slid into one of the padded seats, pulling Jack in beside her.

"I'm scared, too. What I feel for you...I wasn't letting you go. I was coming back for you today."

"Good. I'll try, but there will be times when I'm going to screw up."

"You already said that."

"I mean it. It's really hard for me to trust in this, sweetheart. And hurting you is the last thing I want to do, so don't let me."

She hugged him one more time, then smacked

him on the shoulder. "Now that I know you love me, I'm not cutting you any slack. You're mine."

"I'm yours," he said. He reached into his pocket and pulled out a jeweler's box. He scooted out of the booth and got down on his knee.

Lauren couldn't breathe. He pulled her to the edge of the seat so that he knelt at her feet.

He opened the box and took out a simple white gold band with a large marquis-cut diamond. "Knowing that I'm a frog—that I only pretend to be a prince—will you marry me, Lauren?"

She looked at the ring and the man and knew that if he was the frog then she was the frog princess. She slipped off the bench and knelt beside him, cupping his dear face in her hands.

"Yes."

He kissed her. Held her tightly to him, his fingers fumbling with the ring and sliding it on her finger while his mouth moved on hers. He lifted his head.

"No more Miss Lonely Hearts."

She starting laughing, knowing that her life with Jack was going to be one wild roller-coaster ride. But she wouldn't have it any other way.

Epilogue

The Porsche was decorated with Just Married signs, and Jack and Lauren emerged from a large reception room. Jack carried her in his arms. I liked this part of my new gig the best.

"Nice job, Ray."

I glanced over my shoulder. Didi stood behind me in the late-morning sun. She'd stopped wearing those damned ugly dresses and she looked…aw, hell, I shouldn't even think it, but she looked nice.

"Thanks, babe."

She didn't say anything and I started to feel like a *babbeo*. An idiot. Hell, it wasn't the first time and I knew it wouldn't be the last.

"You know, I think two other couples hooked up from that Mile of Men. Do they count toward my total?" I asked her.

She walked over to me, standing to my right. "Nah, that was too easy."

"You never cut me a break, do you?" I asked, but I didn't mind. This afterlife gig wasn't what I'd ever have imagined for myself, but there was a certain feeling that came from getting these couples together. It made me feel…good.

"I don't want you to take me for granted, babe," she said, slipping her hand into mine.

"Babe?"

"Yeah, babe," she said.

I tried to tug her closer, but she danced away in that teasing way of hers, disappearing in the breeze. I waited until Jack and Lauren drove away, then let myself drift after her.

* * * * *

DYNASTIES: THE ASHTONS

continues in September with

CONDITION OF MARRIAGE
by Emilie Rose

Pregnant by one man, Mercedes Ashton enters
into a marriage of convenience with another
and finds that her in-name-only husband
ignites more passion than she ever imagined!

*Don't miss the drama as Dynasties: The Ashtons
unfolds each month, only in Silhouette Desire.*

If you enjoyed what you just read,
then we've got an offer you can't resist!

Take 2 bestselling love stories FREE!

Plus get a FREE surprise gift!

Clip this page and mail it to Silhouette Reader Service™

IN U.S.A.
3010 Walden Ave.
P.O. Box 1867
Buffalo, N.Y. 14240-1867

IN CANADA
P.O. Box 609
Fort Erie, Ontario
L2A 5X3

YES! Please send me 2 free Silhouette Desire® novels and my free surprise gift. After receiving them, if I don't wish to receive anymore, I can return the shipping statement marked cancel. If I don't cancel, I will receive 6 brand-new novels every month, before they're available in stores! In the U.S.A., bill me at the bargain price of $3.80 plus 25¢ shipping and handling per book and applicable sales tax, if any*. In Canada, bill me at the bargain price of $4.47 plus 25¢ shipping and handling per book and applicable taxes**. That's the complete price and a savings of at least 10% off the cover prices—what a great deal! I understand that accepting the 2 free books and gift places me under no obligation ever to buy any books. I can always return a shipment and cancel at any time. Even if I never buy another book from Silhouette, the 2 free books and gift are mine to keep forever.

225 SDN DZ9F
326 SDN DZ9G

Name	(PLEASE PRINT)	
Address	Apt.#	
City	State/Prov.	Zip/Postal Code

Not valid to current Silhouette Desire® subscribers.

Want to try two free books from another series?
Call 1-800-873-8635 or visit www.morefreebooks.com.

* Terms and prices subject to change without notice. Sales tax applicable in N.Y.
** Canadian residents will be charged applicable provincial taxes and GST.
  All orders subject to approval. Offer limited to one per household.
  ® are registered trademarks owned and used by the trademark owner and or its licensee.

DES04R   ©2004 Harlequin Enterprises Limited

COMING NEXT MONTH

#1675 CONDITION OF MARRIAGE—Emilie Rose
Dynasties: The Ashtons
Abandoned by her lover, pregnant Mercedes Ashton turned to her good friend
Jared Maxwell for help. Jared offered her a marriage of convenience…that
soon flared into unexpected passion. But when the father of Mercedes's
unborn child returned, would her bond with Jared be enough to keep their
marriage together?

#1676 TANNER TIES—Peggy Moreland
The Tanners of Texas
Lauren Tanner was determined to get her life back on track…without the
assistance of her estranged family. When she hired quiet Luke Jordan, she
had no idea the scarred handyman was tied to the Tanners and prepared to use
any method necessary—even seduction—to bring Lauren back into the fold.

**#1677 STRICTLY CONFIDENTIAL ATTRACTION—
Brenda Jackson**
Texas Cattleman's Club: The Secret Diary
Although rancher Mark Hartman's relationship with his attractive secretary,
Alison Lind, had always been strictly professional, it changed when he was
forced to enlist her aid in caring for his infant niece. Now their business
arrangement was venturing into personal—and potentially dangerous—
territory….

#1678 APACHE NIGHTS—Sheri WhiteFeather
Their attraction was undeniable. But neither police detective Joyce Riggs nor
skirting-the-edge-of-the-law Apache Kyle Prescott believed there could be
anything more than passion between them. They decided the answer to their
dilemma was a no-strings affair. That was their first mistake.

#1679 REFLECTED PLEASURES—Linda Conrad
The Gypsy Inheritance
Fashion model Merrill Davis-Ross wanted out of the spotlight and had
reinvented herself as the new plain-Jane assistant of billionaire Texan
Tyson Steele. But her mission to leave her past behind was challenged
when Tyson dared to look beyond Merrill's facade to find the real woman
underneath.

#1680 THE RICH STRANGER—Bronwyn Jameson
Princes of the Outback
When fate stranded Australian playboy Rafe Carlisle on her cattle station,
usually wary Cat McConnell knew she'd never met anyone like this rich
stranger. Because his wild and winning ways tempted her to say yes to night
after night of passion, to a temporary marriage—and even to having his baby!

SDCNM0805